# Earth Under the Martians

## Book 2 of 'The Martians Return'

### Mark Hood

UNSEELIE PRESS

Unseelie Press

ISBN: 1-913442-23-3
ISBN-13: 978-1-913442-23-1

Cover design by GetCovers
GetCovers.com

# Get your free book!

For Martyne, of course.

# Contents

# Chapter One

# Breathing

It had been only a few days since our hard-won victory at the Martian camp. While our losses had been great, our liberation of the prisoners there and the destruction of the base were cause enough for celebration.

The former barracks in Shropshire, which served as our accommodation after our flight from Woking, had now begun to feel more like a home. Previously it had always seemed more like the military base it had once been, occupied as it was by almost exclusively members of the army. With the prisoners being mainly men of science, the place gained a more civilian feeling. If you ignored the overwhelming proportion of men compared to women, you could occasionally deceive yourself into thinking it a small village.

So it was that one evening Amy and I sat in our small quarters, facing one another across a flimsy folding card table, the remnants of our supper congealing on the plates.

Amy has always been swifter to forgive than she is to anger. While I knew that my decision to throw myself into battle still hurt her, that I had latterly put myself into harm's way to rescue her had at least demonstrated the depth of my affection.

"But I would not have doubted your love if you had left things to the professionals," she explained over dinner that evening. "You know that such bombastic heroism has never been the way to my heart. I married a writer, a thinker, and a sensitive man. Had I wanted a warrior or a knight on horseback, I am sure I could acquire one." Her eyes sparkled with mirth and she sipped her tea.

"No doubt," I smiled back, "but rest assured; my days of throwing myself into danger are behind me. Henceforth, I shall be the coward you have always wanted." I raised my teacup in a toast, and we laughed together for the first time in what felt like months.

"So you will not be accompanying Russell and Chambers to Canada?" she asked. "Their hunt for material for bombs and reactors is surely the highest priority?"

"The most involvement I wish with those gentlemen is to break up their occasional fights." I noted Amy's raised eyebrow. "Alright, frequent fights."

"It wasn't long ago that you used that duty as an excuse to charge into peril," she reminded me. "Do you believe they could now survive days on a ship without one of them vanishing overboard at the hands of the other?" Her tone was light, but I sensed a deeper concern.

"Do you want me to go?" I asked. "When only a short while ago I thought you lost, I resolved never to leave you again. We are safe here," I gestured around myself, "Russell's formerly secret base seems overlooked by the Martians, and we can both find a purpose. Indeed, you already have!"

Amy sighed. "The infirmary barely needs my help now, the existing staff can handle the last of the patients without me. Russell's serum has worked miracles."

It was true Russell's team had developed an anti-bacterial compound that halted infection in its tracks, and even the more emaciated and malnourished of the former convicts were fighting their way back to health. It had been engineered from samples of Martian origin, and was presumed to be the key to their survival on this second visit, where they had succumbed to our diseases before.

"There will be more injuries soon enough," I reminded her. "Already there are plans afoot to take the battle back to the Martians if they do not retaliate themselves. Or perhaps you can find employment with the men developing the serum and help countless future patients."

"Or perhaps I can find another path."

"Indeed, rebuilding society will take a variety of skills and talents, and I am sure you can offer a great deal. But why urge me to go? Are you sick of the sight of your husband so soon?" I laughed.

"Of course not, I intend to spend as much time at your side as possible, and that is why you must come with me to Canada."

---

I choked on my tea. Amy sat in silence as I spluttered and coughed, an inscrutable expression upon her face. When I finally regained my breath, I wiped the tears from my eyes and looked deeply into her own.

"Are you serious?" I asked, knowing the answer.

"Absolutely," she replied, "Chambers asked me this afternoon."

"And you said yes?"

"I said I would consult with my spouse before deciding," she replied. "A courtesy you did not grant me, I might remind you."

"But what will you do?"

"Present Russell's serum to our allies, for one."

"He agreed to hand it over?"

"Under duress, I believe. Chambers wants it in his back pocket, in case we need to barter."

"He can do that himself, surely? That man never hesitated from singing his own praises before."

"He has suggested he might remain here to supervise work on his weaponised germs," she replied. "And wants someone to act on his behalf."

"Chambers, then; he's more than capable."

"He asked me to do it, as someone with medical experience. Besides, the expedition may need a nurse, and it would be foolish to leave the infirmary here understaffed by sending one of their number."

"So stay here and fill that space," I protested. "You have proven your worth and need not gallivant half way around the world to prove it again."

"So says the man who insisted on joining a military assault. What of mankind's foremost chronicler of the Martian invasions? Will he sit out the first strategic mission of our retaliation?"

"If it means keeping him and his wife safe from harm, absolutely!"

She gave a hollow laugh. "As if anywhere is safe in these times!"

"You know damn well what I meant," I snapped. "A trip across the Atlantic is foolhardy enough, without considering the situation in Canada might be even worse than it is here. We have no contact with them, the Martians may have exterminated them! And need I remind you, we are currently in Shropshire, practically as far from the sea as one can be. The trip to find a boat might be an even greater peril than the voyage itself!"

"We have an opportunity, with the Martian forces in this area disrupted," she countered. "Radio communication is spotty, but Chambers assures me he has spoken to men in Canada who survived. Bristol is less than a day's travel, the port there will furnish us a boat."

"Not one suitable for a journey as far as you propose!"

Amy remained calm even as my voice rose. "It will take us to a ship moored offshore. One that regularly plies the seas between us and the Americas, and can convey us safely to our destination."

"You've thought of everything," I conceded.

"Chambers has," she replied. "And Russell, although I would be foolish to take his pronouncements at face value. But you must concede that when both men agree, it is a good sign that there is some truth in their opinions."

"It quite seems as if you have made up your mind," I folded my arms. "So why even consult me?"

"Because, unlike you, I value my spouse's opinion." She held up a hand against my protests. "Perhaps that is unfair, but you did not consider it when I begged you not to risk yourself."

"And you will consider it if I likewise beg you now?" I scoffed.

"Of course."

"Then do not go. I wish you safe and sound with me."

A deafening rising and falling tone interrupted our discussion. For an instant we sat motionless, unable to understand what we were hearing, before realisation dawned.

"An attack!" we both cried at the same moment. I leapt to my feet, my chair tumbling over behind me as I raced to Amy's side. Together, we sprinted from the room and joined the scurrying mass of bodies heading outside.

The evening was not yet fully dark, but after the lamp-lit interior of our room, my eyes struggled to pierce the gloom. Amy passed me my overcoat, which she had grabbed on our way out, and slipped on her own against the early evening chill.

Barely a breath was audible, as every soul present strained to hear some evidence of what had disturbed our dinner. The soldiers arrayed along the walls of the camp levelled their rifles, and the synchronised sound of their bolts snapping into place made us jump. A nervous laugh came from one member of the terrified crowd before they quickly stifled it.

I doubt I could have seen anything over the wall that encircled us. Should a Martian have got close enough to be visible over the ramparts, our lookouts would have failed us. The siren continued its baleful song from the watchtower before falling into a silence that enveloped the entire camp.

"Ready!" came a cry from the wall. A flare rocketed into the sky, arcing over and away from the camp along the main road. It crackled into life, casting an ominous red glow over our upturned faces. I trusted it was illuminating an empty vista, allowing a false alarm to be declared, and the all-clear sounded. The lookouts had been twitchy the last few days.

"Aim!"

So there was something there. Something threatening, something which needed to be repelled. Perhaps, I dared to hope, it was not a Martian. Maybe it was a contingent of men, refugees, or escaped from a camp somehow, seeking shelter. But then why would the guards aim their rifles at them? Jumpy or not, surely no man would not repeat the atrocity I had witnessed the last time people came for aid?

My worst fears were realised when a familiar sound cracked open the sky.

"*Ullah!*"

The crowd immediately panicked. The military, to their credit, never wavered on their walls. Rifles aimed unerringly at the distant intruder, they stood their ground, awaiting the order. Amy and I clung tighter tightly against the jostling of the purposeless mob our neighbours had become. Most of them were the prisoners we had liberated a few days before, and I could well forgive them for their reaction to the thought of being captured once more.

"Fire!"

The crack of rifle fire echoed around the camp, flashes of light illuminating every inch of the barricades, and every stoic face positioned there. A hand clamped upon my shoulder, and I spun angrily, ready to defend myself from my unseen assailant. I looked into the terrified eyes of Chambers, who spoke quietly but firmly to my wife and I.

"We have to go. Now."

## Chapter Two

# Uprooted

The panicking mob had now found a purpose and was fleeing to the rear of the camp. Chambers, accompanied by his wife and children, led us along after them. At the small rear gate, a detachment of soldiers funnelled the stampede through the narrow exit. They urged people not to form large groups and pointed each handful of terrified civilians in a different direction. One nodded curtly at Chambers and ushered us through together.

"We have no supplies, none of our belongings," I protested.

"There is no time," Chambers replied. "I have a few necessities." He brandished a hold-all bag, and I noted that his wife also carried one. They had clearly been expecting something like this, unlike Amy and me.

"Where are we going?" Amy asked. "Is there safety nearby?"

Chambers' lips were tight. "We should focus on where we do not wish to be, first. Where we can go later is a problem for another time."

The group of us hurried in silence away from the camp, making for the relative cover of the tree-line. The pines that had stood for decades now leaned against one another under the weight of the red weed that choked them, but they would offer us concealment and some modicum of safety. As we neared the forest, I glanced back over my shoulder at the camp as an all-too-familiar silhouette rose above the horizon.

The Martian fighting machine was already brandishing the heat-ray generator at the end of a long tentacle, and snapped it to bear on the watchtower, silencing the cries of the men within. Flames sprang up wherever it touched, and more screams carried over to us in the still air of the evening.

"Come on," Amy urged in a whisper, and I followed her into the gloom of the overgrown woods.

We huddled together in the pitch blackness, glad of our overcoats, and listened to the crackling of flames from our former home. The cries of the poor souls who hadn't escaped had ceased as abruptly as they had begun, and I shivered from more than the cold. Chamber's wife Mary kept the children quiet, playing cat's cradle and similar silent games to occupy them and keep them from considering their situation. I wished that my own mind was so easily distracted.

Amy pressed herself more tightly against my side, and I threw an arm around her to hold her close. Words of comfort wouldn't come, and besides, to speak now might invite doom upon us all. Questions burned inside me. Had Chambers made a plan? He and his wife had prepared for a rapid evacuation, so I had to hope that he did. I cursed my optimism; our recent success had led me to think we were safe—had I not just reassured Amy?—and I had neglected to consider any other possibility. Had Russell also escaped? I might not have liked the man, but his research offered the best hope of victory, whether through explosive devices or bacterial means. We had made few enough friends at the camp that I could barely even think of the names of anyone else I might fear for.

I do not know how long we cowered there, whether minutes or hours, but eventually the thumping of the tripod's feet retreated into the distance, and we dared to breathe more easily once more.

I stood, stretching out cramped muscles and creaky joints, and I retraced our steps back to the edge of our wooded refuge. The camp was ablaze, thick black smoke roiling into the sky to blot out the stars. Of the Martian there was no sign, though for all I knew it might be hiding in the smoke waiting for some foolhardy man to poke his head out.

"What do you see?" Chambers' voice behind me caused me to leap almost out of my skin, so loud it seemed after our period of silence.

Once my heart no longer threatened to break free of my ribcage, I whispered back. "Nothing, but more destruction." I felt Amy's hand slide into mine and I clasped her fingers.

We retreated into the woods, where Mrs Chambers broke out a small tin of peach slices. She opened it awkwardly with a pocket-knife and passed it around our circle. One by one we extracted a slice, careful of the sharp edges of the can, and nibbled away at the sweet flesh. I can't deny my spirits lifted slightly at such a simple pleasure.

Chambers lit a small lamp, turned it as low as it could go, and urged us to sit in a circle around it to shield as much light as possible. The shadows cast by the guttering flame loomed eerily about us, and I focused instead on the faces of my companions.

Chambers pulled a map from his bag and spread it out next to the lamp. "The camp is destroyed, and so we must find shelter elsewhere. I believe we have two choices." He stabbed a finger at the map. "This is where we are," he said. "And this," — another stab — "is the government shelter in Wiltshire."

"How far?" Amy asked.

"About a hundred miles," he replied.

"What is the second option?" I asked.

Another jab of the finger, left of the last spot. "Bristol. About the same distance."

"And what is there?" I feared I already knew the answer.

"A boat. Several boats, in fact, but in particular..."

I finished his sentence. "One to take us to Canada."

"I assume," I said, "that you intend for us to head to Wiltshire." I looked over at his wife and children. "A sea voyage in these times would be no place for a young family."

Chambers nodded. "Mary will take care of the children there, while we regroup and provision ourselves for the journey."

"And it would be good to reunite with my brother, also," I pointed out.

"So why is there even a need to make a choice?" Amy asked.

"We have no contact with the site in Wiltshire any longer. All was well yesterday, when we last spoke, but I have no radio gear. If the Martians attacked them simultaneously, we would have no way of knowing."

"Is that likely?" I asked, fear for my brother gnawing at my heart.

"We cannot discount it. They found us easily enough, and perhaps they were listening in on our radio signals and triangulated them. They were blocking them before, so we rarely transmitted. With the break in their coverage, we might have led them to us."

"We should have taken precautions," Amy said. "Foreseen this and avoided the dangers."

"We should," Chambers agreed. "But we didn't. I only re-alised our folly when my mind turned to pondering how they had tracked us down."

"So it might be for the best that we don't possess radio gear," I noted.

"Being on the move should prevent them following us, but I am glad not to run the risk. Besides, if anyone took a radio from the camp before they left, we are unlikely to catch up with them. If they have learned the fate of the government base, we shall not be any the wiser."

"So you think it safer to head to Bristol, in case Wiltshire has been compromised?" I asked.

"I think it merits discussion," Chambers replied. "We were in contact with a vessel stationed offshore, out of the Mar-tians' range. We agreed if we lost contact, that they would send a boat ashore once a week to look for us, and take us aboard. Even if the Martians know where they were, they won't have any way to reach them, so they will be a safe refuge. And they will know what has happened in Wiltshire."

"If anything has," Amy said. "You are quick to count them out."

A gentle cough interrupted us. All of us spun to look at Mary, her two children clinging to her skirts.

"Might I venture an opinion?" she asked. I believe it was the first time I had heard her speak. "The route to both begins in the same direction, does it not?" Her husband nodded, glancing at the map. "Then let's get underway and make our decision when we come to the fork in the road. Perhaps we will meet with someone who can furnish us more information, or circumstances will decide for us. In any case, these two" — she indicated her children — "won't be getting any less sleepy."

I was glad of her clear thinking, as evidently my capacity for rational thought was another thing I had lost when the camp was attacked.

I had never travelled with small children, Amy and I having never been blessed with our own, and my brother a bachelor. Under normal circumstances, I would have found the slow pace tedious, but in our current situation, it was downright infuriating.

The children, Maureen and Stanley, were old enough to walk unaided, though slowly. Had they been smaller, we might take turns carrying them and increased our speed, but they limited us to the speed of their short legs. Their endurance was also less than our own. By the time we needed to take our first rest break, barely an hour had passed, and I estimated we had travelled only two miles or fewer. The first glow of dawn was already threatening in the east, and I could only hope that we were far enough from the camp to avoid discovery.

Please understand I do not hold this against them, they could no more help their age and ability than I could control my anxiety and disquiet at our sluggish progress. But compared to the pace of the flight from Woking that Amy and I had undertaken, this was disconcerting.

At the second rest stop, perhaps three miles from our hiding spot, I took Chambers aside. I explained my fear that this pace would mean our journey might take over a week to complete.

"That would put us at greater risk of discovery, the sooner we are in shelter, the better for all of us."

"Push on ahead," he said. "You can scout the way for us and make it to safety more quickly without us slowing you down."

"Not a chance. Fate has decided that we are in this together."

"You can leave notes for us on the way, perhaps even discover the fate of the site in Wiltshire. Should they have fallen, you can wait for us on the road and save us that leg of the journey at least."

His argument made sense, but I could not consider leaving the Chambers family to make their own way while we strode off ahead. Even if I had allowed myself to be swayed by Chambers' arguments, Amy would never have countenanced it. I glanced over to where she stood with the children, amusing them with games and riddles to give the poor, overwhelmed Mrs Chambers some respite from their constant demands.

"We stick together," I said. "But we need a faster means of transport, and one that is easier on your children." I thought for a moment. "Bicycles would be ideal: small, quiet and easily concealed if we needed to hide. I doubt we shall find any here, not enough for us all."

"And I have never ridden one, nor Mary or the children."

"A cart, then. And a horse to pull it, if one survives." I checked the map. "There is a farm not far off our route, which might furnish us with what we need."

A plan formulated, we then informed the ladies of our decision. Chambers and I would investigate the farm while the women and children pressed on. If they feared for their safety, they could find shelter in some hiding place. A temporary separation to avoid a longer one, I explained. Mary protested at first, reluctant to remain without her husband's protection, but Amy assured her that no harm would come to them.

"There are no wild animals to fear, and we have seen no sign of anyone so far, let alone brigands or highwaymen. And our valiant menfolk will be away for so short a period you will not notice their absence, except perhaps by the peace and quiet it will afford us." She smiled, and once again I marvelled at her strength under pressure. She did not mention the Martian threat, and fortunately Mary did not either; Amy knew as well as I did that should one appear, the presence or absence of myself and Chambers would make no difference to the outcome. She and I drew aside to allow Chambers and his wife some privacy for their goodbyes.

"I trust that this does not count as unnecessary bravery," I said. "I promised you a coward, after all."

She smiled, but her countenance returned to serious all too quickly. "About our argument," she began.

I shook my head. "Consider it forgotten," I said. "Events have forced our hand, and we shall go where the road takes us."

"But we must still decide our destination," Amy protested.

"As Mrs Chambers so cleverly pointed out, we cannot know that until we get closer. We shall decide when the time is right."

I kissed her cheek and embraced her, and Chambers and I set off along the unmade road that led to Stoke Farm.

## Chapter Three

# Trudging

The narrow road weaved its way through the countryside, twisting around rocks and trees that had been too much trouble to move. We had little visibility of the surrounding scenery, the hedges on either side now swallowed by mounds of the red weed blocking the view. The absence of the usual sounds of nature lent a spooky air to our journey, I would have given anything to hear a familiar bird singing. Despite the watery sunshine, we felt quite oppressed and gloomy as we walked, and our pace picked up in response.

A foul stench arose as we neared our destination, that of death and decay. At the gates of the farm, we steeled ourselves against what we might encounter and reassured one another that it had been the right decision not to bring the women and children with us. Traversing the farmyard revealed the source of the smell: dead cattle in the milking shed. Their bodies had all but rotted away, the last shreds of flesh on their bones green and slimy with decay. My stomach lurched, and we turned away to seek what we needed.

"Hello?" Chambers called nervously. I jumped, the sudden interruption to the silence around us feeling somehow rude. "Anyone here?"

"If there were, would they not have seen to their cows?" I asked.

"We are about to steal from these people, it is only right to ask first if we can offer them the chance to come with us," he explained.

No reply came. We investigated the farmhouse, the ivy that had climbed its walls now dead and covered by the invasive weed from Mars, and found no sign of anyone. Dust covered every surface indoors—if someone had been here, they were long gone now. At my suggestion Chambers began checking through their larder to see if any food was still edible, while I went in search of transport.

The barn at the other side of the yard was intact, a sturdy padlock securing a thick wooden bar across the front. I took this as a good sign that the contents were undisturbed, though I spotted a loose plank to one side of the door. Pulling it back, I could poke my head inside. Through the gloom, I thought I spotted a wagon of some sort, though the state of it was impossible to discern in the darkness. I headed back to the house, checking the horizon on all sides for any sign of the Martians. We saw none, but thick black storm clouds were rolling in from the west. We would need to find shelter before the weather turned.

Chambers had found a few tins and a handful of jars of pickled goods, which we split between our backpacks. He and I searched in vain for the key to the barn, until we decided the owner must have had it with him when he had left, or was taken. I recalled seeing a wood-axe near the cowshed, and together we worked to break in to the barn.

Removing the loose plank was easy, but we realised that we'd never be able to open a hole wide enough for any cart to exit.

Our focus had to be the regular entrance. A few blows of the axe did nothing to the padlock besides scuffing its surface, so we turned our attention to the wooden bar across the doors. I found a pleasant rhythm in the lifting and swinging of the axe, and the bite of the blade into the wood, and before long I was sweating. I handed over to Chambers for a spell and took off my jacket. While he took his turn, I checked the water pump that stood in one corner of the yard, and found it was still supplying fresh water, ice-cold, and we drank deeply before refilling our water canteens.

"Should we shelter here?" I asked Chambers when he paused for breath. "If we can retrieve this cart before the women get too far, we might make it back here before that storm."

He surveyed the horizon and shook his head. "I doubt we'd make it in time, and I'd rather not they had to endure this stench. The stables are foul as well, I suspect the black smoke killed all the animals while the farmer fled."

"Could we not burn the bodies?" I asked, "Perhaps the buildings themselves?"

"It would doubtless spread to the house, and we'd be without shelter. Not to mention the attention it would draw. With luck we'll find canvas or something in here to fashion a tent from, if we are not fortunate enough to find shelter on the road."

I took my next turn with the axe and finally the bar yielded. With a last check around us, paranoid that our noisy activities had attracted attention, we stepped into the gloom.

Even with the doors flung wide, it was so dim inside that I stumbled over an unseen bucket and almost measured my length on the hay-strewn floor. We continued our exploration with greater caution after that, aware of the peril that any injury would place us all in. Without horses, it would fall upon us to pull the cart, and we would need to be unhurt.

The cart was sturdy and well maintained, and Chambers and I pulled it out into the fading sunlight of the farm yard. It rolled easily and quietly, and we checked it over. It was more than adequately sized for all of us to fit inside, which would at least prevent us from spending another night on the hard earth. The wheels were large and iron-rimmed, sturdy enough for the journey we planned to undertake. Two long poles jutted from the front, and a harness stretched between them; if we had found a horse, we would have had no difficulty engaging it to pull us along. As it was, that duty would fall to Chambers and me.

Mindful of the oncoming storm, we worked hastily and loaded the cart with the provisions Chambers had dug out of the pantry, a pot from the kitchen, some clothing we found in the farm house along with various ropes, blocks, and other items from the barn we thought might come in handy. Any guilt we felt at stealing from these hardworking folk was tempered by the knowledge that they almost certainly had no need for their belongings now. We picked up a couple of straw bales to use as bedding and insulation against the night, and hefted them into our transport.

A vast canvas sheet was the last of our discoveries, and together Chambers and I strapped it down over the bed of the cart with ropes. Hopefully it would serve as enough protection from the elements, and since the sides of the cart rose about eighteen inches above the bed, it meant that we could crawl in under its shelter and be safe from prying eyes as well as from the rain.

Chambers lifted one trace, I took up the other, and we hauled the cart across the cobblestones and into the darkening evening. We exchanged a glance, and I knew he was thinking the same as I, but would never say it. We increased our pace, keen to catch up to our families before something could happen to them.

Chapter Four

# Travelling

Fear of the storm, terror of being followed and concern over the safety of the women and children drove us to push ourselves as hard as we could, and in a little over an hour, we caught up with the rest of our party. The rain had overtaken us all, and while Chambers and I had equipped ourselves with waterproofs from the farm, our wives and the children were reliant only on their overcoats. By the time we reached them, they were all drenched to the bone.

We parked the cart at the edge of the road, placing rocks beneath the wheels to prevent it rolling. The children clambered into the back, followed by the women, and they changed into the dry clothing we had scavenged while Chambers and I stood guard outside. Once they pronounced themselves decent, we stripped off our raincoats and climbed in to join them.

"Did you not find any towels?" Amy asked. Chambers and I looked guiltily at each other; we had been so proud of our planning and foraging, but had overlooked that simplest of thoughts. "Never send a man to do a woman's job," she joked. "We made do, but you may not have a dry set of clothes to change into tomorrow," she explained. The shirts we had gathered for ourselves lay damp and bunched up in a corner of the space.

"Did you at least find a tin opener?" Mary enquired, and Chambers' face brightened as he produced two of them from his pocket. The ladies set to work opening tins and dishing up a meagre supper for us all.

As we ate, the rain drummed down on the canvas. Fortunately, it held the water at bay for now, although from time to time it would pool in a low spot and encroach upon our living area. Whoever was nearest would push upwards, displacing the water and sending it over the side of the cart. The children thought this a grand sport, and we were all glad of the distraction.

With the endless rain we could not start a fire, not that it would have been wise. We still feared discovery, and Chambers and I resolved to take turns watching and listening out for any disturbance. The women also offered to take their turn, but Chambers refused to hear of it. I knew I would not persuade Amy, and so I agreed we would allow them their turn, while winking at Chambers to let him know I had no intention of waking them. Such subterfuge would only work tonight, however, as she would no doubt insist on taking the first watch tomorrow, but at least we could spare them the burden for now. I took the first shift, promising to wake him when a few hours had passed.

I woke with a start. The monotonous rain had lulled my tired body and mind into slumber without my even noticing, and I had neglected my duty to our group. I sat bolt upright, or at least tried to; my face pressed into the rough canvas and panic overwhelmed me for a moment before I remembered I was beneath our cover.

A quiet chuckle came from the corner. I leant up on my elbows to find Amy stifling a laugh with her hand.

"I knew full well you would not wake me," she whispered. "But the rain letting up disturbed me enough to rouse me, not to mention your snoring. I gather you ended your lookout a little earlier than planned."

I protested, as quietly but vehemently as I could, but she smiled.

"You needed your rest, and no harm befell us. I doubt you were asleep for long."

"What time is it?" I asked.

"Almost dawn," she replied. "I let Chambers sleep too. I decided our cart-horses should be well rested for the day's journey. Now that you are awake, though, I shall begin on breakfast."

I needed to relieve myself and making my excuses, wandered over to the trees beside the road. The grass was still wet from the night's storm, and sunrise was insinuating itself over the hills in the east, making the red weed glisten disconcertingly in the first light. I could see well enough to make my way to privacy, and I did what I needed to do without disaster. On my way back, however, a tightening dread overcame me. Something was wrong, something dreadful, and it took me a few moments to realise what it was.

There was still no sound. The dawn chorus of birds should have been overwhelming at this hour, the rustle of small animals seeking shelter before the predators came to find them should have been everywhere. This place was devoid of all animal life, apart from the six of us. I shuddered and hurried back to our cart and the welcoming arms of my wife.

Breakfast came from tins once again, but at least this time we could warm the contents. Chambers found enough dry wood to make a small campfire, and with the dawn all around us, we no longer feared being spotted from a great distance. We kept the fire well ventilated to avoid smoke and watched it like hawks. Even the small flames licking around the pot were heartening to see, and helped drive the last of the damp from our clothing. With full bellies and dry boots, we set about continuing our journey.

The cart improved our speed, as we were no longer limited to the walking pace of young children. But there were times I cursed its very existence. On level ground, it was a delight to pull; Chambers and I had slung ropes between the traces instead of harnesses, and could simply exert gentle pressure with our shoulders to propel our vehicle along smoothly. But the way was never level for long, and even the smallest incline needed careful preparation. Uphill was bad enough, the weight of the cart threatening to drag us back down if we relented in our efforts. On one or two gradients, the women had to leave the cart to lighten our load, and even push from the back to assist us. But more dangerous were the downhill sections.

Ideally we would let the cart gather speed downhill to carry it up the next inclination, but the only means of steering the cart was for Chambers and me to move from side to side in the road, the front axle of the cart being linked to the traces we pulled. So if the cart picked up any speed, we had to keep up with it lest we lose control and the wagon pitch itself into the side of the road. More than once we found ourselves hauling back on the ropes, our boots slithering down the road, terrified of the cart overtaking us and rolling its huge iron-rimmed wheels over one or both of us. Amy and Mary could not remain inside for these downhill stretches either, as the weight of the cart was all but overwhelming on its own. For all Amy's talk of the cart-horses being well rested, the women got little benefit from the vehicle.

But around mid-morning we encountered a relatively long stretch of gentle descent, and could simply allow the cart to rattle along under its own weight with only the occasional nudge from one of us to keep it aligned. This section of road had been well-travelled before the invasion and deep grooves worn by previous users helped keep the wheels on track. Amy hung our wet clothing of the day before on a line across the rear of the cart, and it billowed out behind us drying in the warming sun. Despite everything, we felt more optimistic when we broke for lunch. We sat on the bales of hay in the cart's rear and munched on cold meat and pickles.

I voiced the thought which had been troubling me all morning. "It's curious we have met no-one on the road yet. There were many people escaped from our camp, and we should have met some of them before now."

"It has been slow going," Chambers pointed out between mouthfuls. "Even with the cart, and even more so before we found it. They will be well ahead of us by now." My face must have shown my despair. "That being said, we have made almost ten miles this morning," he reassured me. "The map shows no major changes in elevation, and so I believe we might manage another fifteen this afternoon. Assuming we are all up to the challenge?"

A chorus of agreement met his question.

"Excellent. Then let us..." He didn't finish the sentence, and stared behind me, his face pale. We all turned to face whatever had startled him and saw the unmistakable outline of a Martian tripod stalking past.

# Chapter Five

# Sighting

The Martian was perhaps a quarter-mile distant, heading from the north. If it held its path, it would cross the road we were on a mere few hundred yards ahead of us. For an instant, we all sat frozen in place, before the spell broke and I scrambled to my feet.

"Sit still," Amy hissed. She pulled at my trouser leg, and I obediently sat back down as slowly as I could manage on my shaking legs. "It may not see us," she whispered. She was right, it was probably not searching for us, and would only investigate if something drew its attention. Fleeing would certainly draw its ire upon us, and we could never hope to outpace it. While every thought in my head was screaming at me to run, every muscle in my body locked with the effort of sitting still. My breath sounded so loud in my nostrils I was sure the Martian would hear it. The pounding of my heart seemed to shake my whole body so violently I was surprised the cart itself was not vibrating in sympathy.

Painfully slowly, to my eyes, the Martian picked its way through the fields and over the hedges as it drew closer to the road. Abruptly, it stopped, the rearmost of its legs in the act of lifting from the ground. For a moment, it balanced there, before the leg moved back into position and it settled sturdily upon its tripod base.

"It's stopped," Mary stated the obvious in a tiny whisper. "Why has it stopped?"

Had it seen us? Heard us? Panic flooded my soul; I wanted to flee, to take flight and run until my lungs burst, rather than face another of these monsters. In that moment, I would have left my wife and friends, not to mention their children, behind me in my terror, had I succumbed to the impulse. Somehow I found the strength to remain, grasping Amy's hand so tightly she winced at the pain.

The fighting machine's head snapped towards us. I felt Amy jerk, sensed the slight movement of the cart as every one of us tensed for the inevitable. Then, miraculously, improbably, it moved again, looking downwards towards a point between us and itself. The lower part of its carapace slid open to allow the handling tentacles to emerge, and two of them darted towards the ground near its feet. We heard a scream, almost silenced by the distance, before one arm lifted back up, holding a struggling figure in its coils. More shouts and cries went up, and it lifted another figure. It deposited these men in a basket slung below the main body of the machine, and the tentacles descended once again.

Breathlessly, we watched as almost a dozen men and women were snatched up and caged. The Martian swung about this way and that, picking up everyone it saw until, evidently satisfied that it had captured them all, it set off moving again and continued south. It crossed the road, and without so much as glancing in our direction, continued on. The cries and pleading of the captives it had taken became quieter as it went until we heard them no more.

My head pounded, my muscles ached, and now that it was safe to move once more, I found myself immobile. The children began crying, and Mary hurried to reassure them we were not in danger. Chambers let out a huge sigh, winced as he stretched his tired limbs, and looked at me grimly.

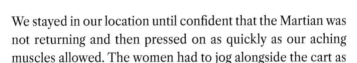

We stayed in our location until confident that the Martian was not returning and then pressed on as quickly as our aching muscles allowed. The women had to jog alongside the cart as we endeavoured to clear the point where the fighting machine had crossed our route.

Eventually we decided we must have put enough distance between ourselves and any remaining danger, and stopped to catch our breath. We drank deeply from our water supply, our hurried flight and the tension causing our mouths to dry almost to the point we could not speak. While we recovered our energy as best we could, Amy spotted a curl of smoke rising above the trees that lined the road ahead.

"The heat-ray?" I wondered aloud.

"No, it's too small for it to be from that," Chambers declared. "Even after the storm dampened everything, that thing's powerful enough to set acres on fire at one touch."

"A campfire," I suggested.

"They're foolish if they're letting it smoke that much," Amy said. "Drawing attention like that."

Chambers examined the map. "We have to go that way," he said. "There are no branches from this road until we're well beyond it. We can either wait until they extinguish it and move on, or press ahead and warn them."

I knew what I wanted to do. "The longer we wait, the more danger they're in, and by extension us. There's no cover here to hide."

Amy agreed with my assessment, Chambers had no objections and Mary accepted our decision without a word. We urged the women back into the cart and resumed our journey.

It was only a half-mile or so later that we saw the source of the smoke. To our surprise, it was coming from the chimney of a cottage in the middle of a tiny village. Most of the other houses were destroyed by collapse or by fire, and the burned-out carcass of an army lorry stood in the road.

"We have to warn them," Amy urged me, so I strode up to the front door and knocked forcefully. A muttering and grumbling came from inside before the door was flung open to reveal a wrinkle-faced bent old man leaning on a stick as gnarled as his hands.

"Oh, hello!" His greeting was so warm in contrast to his sullen-sounding complaints before the door opened that it quite threw me off my stride.

Amy stepped up. "Good afternoon. You should be careful with that fire, you know, there're Martians in the area. You don't want to draw attention."

"Oh, but I do," he grinned. "How else can I bring fine folks like you to my door? Come in, rest yourselves. And you have children too, how wonderful! Bring them in, bring them in." He stepped aside and beckoned us to enter.

A fire burned in the grate, and an old woman sat in a tattered armchair so close to it she must have risked singeing herself. Even from the doorway, I could feel the wall of heat that it emitted, and loosened my jacket.

"Excuse me not getting up," she croaked, "my old legs aren't what they used to be. In my younger years, I was up and down the hills around here all day, now I just tend the fires and look after our visitors." She threw another log onto the hearth, which blazed and spattered.

"But, the Martians," I stammered. "What of the Martians?"

"Oh, we don't trouble them, and they don't trouble us," she said. "Arthur, go fetch something for our guests, run along."

"Yes, Mabel." The old man hobbled into the kitchen, from where a clattering and banging erupted. I moved towards the sound, wishing to help, but the woman urged me to sit.

"He's fine, don't worry. It always makes his day when new people stop in, gives him a chance to show off."

Amy and I settled on a sagging sofa as far from the fire as we could manage. Even above the scent of burning wood, I could detect another aroma, one that I could not place at first. The Chambers family took up positions around the scuffed dining table. We sat awkwardly for a moment before Amy could not hold her tongue any longer.

"But why the fire?"

"My bones don't half feel the cold. You'll see when you get to my age. Assuming you're lucky enough to get there, of course. Nothing's for certain in these times."

I shuddered and asked about the smoke. "Your husband, Arthur, he said it was to bring people in."

As if summoned, he emerged from the kitchen, his walking stick in one hand and an overloaded tray balanced on the other. Amy leapt to her feet to assist him, but he shooed her aside with his cane, though not unkindly. He slid the tray onto the dining table, and began unloading cups and saucers, teaspoons and a steaming teapot covered with a knitted cosy. The final item was hidden under a shining silvery dome, which he removed with a flourish, revealing a small mountain of angel cakes. That had been the unfamiliar scent, one from a life I had long thought over.

The children's eyes widened at the sight of these, and they eagerly asked their mother if they might be allowed to eat them.

"Go on," Arthur said, "that's why we have them. We take in travellers and refugees like yourselves, give them food and drink or whatever else we can spare, and then send them on their way."

"We have a few chickens in the back garden," Mabel added, "for the eggs, you know. And enough butter for a good while. As for flour, the farmer just got his wheat harvest in before they came for him" — she made the sign of the cross — "and so we have plenty to go around."

Arthur poured the tea, and we all dined on the small, sweet cakes. They were the finest I had ever tasted, something I'm sure was not only due to how long it had been since I'd eaten anything like them. They transported me back to my childhood, sitting on a stiff-backed chair at my grandmother's and being plied with all manner of homemade sweets and pastries.

"You're too kind," I said between mouthfuls. The children had polished off their first cake each, and were now hungrily eyeing the last few on the plate. With a chuckle, Arthur placed one ceremoniously in front of each of them and took his seat next to his wife.

"So where are you headed?" he asked.

"Wiltshire," Chambers replied, "in search of more of our colleagues." He briefly outlined the fall of our camp and our enforced flight. "Have any of them passed through here?"

"We had a few two days ago," Mabel confirmed, "telling the same story as you. Was it two days, or three now?" she asked Arthur.

"Three, I think," he replied.

"Two days," she said. "About eight of them, in sore need of food and water. Some of them didn't even have decent boots, you can just imagine the blisters they had. Not like you fine folks, you almost look prepared for a long journey."

"We had bags ready to go," Chambers agreed.

"Thank you so much for your hospitality," I said, rising. "But we cannot impose any longer, we only stopped by to check if you were safe and sound here."

"Nonsense," Arthur said, motioning me to sit back down. "Stay, rest yourselves. There's no rush."

I hesitated, the draw of a warm fire was tempting, no matter how stifling this room was becoming. Against that I weighed the risk of lingering so long as close to where we had last seen the Martians. No matter what these two believed, that fire had to be a risk. In these times, fires were rare enough that we would not be the only curious investigators.

"We have a long journey ahead of us," I insisted, "and should continue it while the weather allows. Thank you once again. When we reach our destination, we shall endeavour to send you some assistance in return, perhaps arrange for you to join us in safety."

"Oh, we won't be going anywhere," Arthur said, struggling to his feet. "And neither will you."

## Chapter Six

# Flight

He turned the key in the lock of the front door and pocketed it. "You'll wait here until they arrive, and then we'll hand you over. Should buy us some more goodwill."

"There's no dealing with the Martians," I said. "Any bargain you think you have is an illusion."

"They've spared us so far," Mabel said. "You see, they need people for their... whatever it is they're doing, and rather someone else than us."

"They're working people to death," Chambers cried. "You're only here because they realise you're too weak to last long." I realised he was right, but that didn't explain why the Martians hadn't taken them as food, or just used the black smoke or heat-ray to wipe them out. Maybe they did appreciate the help, and found it convenient to have a location where survivors gathered together for easier collection.

"Let us out," I demanded. "Allow us to continue on our way and we will send help for you, as I promised."

"Fat chance," Arthur sneered. "You'll send your soldiers and shoot us dead."

"I promise you," I placed my hand over my heart. "Despite your betrayal."

"At least let the children go," Amy asked. "Please, have you no compassion? You can't be considering handing them over to those... monsters."

Chambers' children were clinging to their mother, their cake forgotten. I prayed they didn't understand the genuine danger we were in and were just reacting to the agitation of the surrounding adults.

"Compassion?" Mabel pulled herself out of her chair and walked, in clear pain, up to Amy until they were nose to nose. "Where was compassion when they killed our son? When our grandchildren died screaming?"

"You'd still help the Martians after they did that?" I gasped.

"Martians, pah," Albert spat. "It was your lot, the army, the government, that killed them."

Mary let out a small cry, and the children clung to her ever tighter.

"Might as well have been you yourself," Albert said, staring me in the eye. "One of your lorries was passing through, and a Martian appeared on the road. The soldiers stopped, jumped out, and started shooting. My son pleaded with the driver to take us all out of there, away from the fighting, but he wouldn't do it. So Jacob took it into his own hands."

Mabel backed away from Amy, tears springing to her eyes.

Albert gripped her shoulder and kissed her on the cheek. "He was lifting the kids into the back when that soldier spotted him. He was meant to be fighting the Martian, but he shot down our son without even a second thought. Shot him in the back in front of his own children. Can you imagine?"

"They were screaming," Mabel continued. "I tried to get to them, but another one of those infernal soldiers held me back." She wiped tears from her cheek as she sank back into her chair. "They were dragging our grandchildren out of the lorry, grabbing them and just yanking them out. They flung them into the dirt like garbage."

Both of them were crying and my own eyes were prickling with tears. I could imagine the scene all too vividly, and my stomach turned in cartwheels as I imagined Chambers' children in the same situation.

"Then the Martian…" Albert began, before sobs convulsed through him. He regained his composure with a few deep breaths. "The enemy they had been meant to fight came and burned the lorry, and the soldiers, and…" He trailed off, shoulders shaking with grief.

"We were spared, somehow," Mabel whispered. "I think they knew we'd suffered enough. So we brought them offerings, signal them when we had visitors." She gestured towards the fire.

The strange-burning log in the fireplace.

"Colours the smoke," she confirmed. "They're never far away."

"You're insane," Chambers cried. "They didn't spare you because of your loss, they just didn't care. I'm sorry for what you went through, I am, but that story will have been repeated ten thousand times across the country. The Martians are our enemy, not each other."

"You would rob us of justice?" Arthur shouted.

"That's not justice," I protested. "It's vengeance. And aimed at the wrong people. We had nothing to do with that tragedy." Memories of the massacre at the camp gates surfaced unbidden, and my throat seized up, making further argument impossible.

"We're not waiting here," Amy said, and nudged me in the side. I caught her eye, and she tilted her head almost imperceptibly towards Arthur and the door. I knew she meant me to charge him, to steal back the key, and I nodded as subtly as I could manage. He would be easy enough to overpower, and he was unarmed. But something held me back.

These people had suffered so much, lost everything they cared about. I could never forget the terrible act I had been forced to perform during the first invasion, and if I had witnessed Amy's death, what might I have been driven to do? But no, I had been in fear of my life, it had not been revenge or anger that drove my hand.

Albert dug into his pocket for a handkerchief, and I saw my chance. I launched myself towards him; a few quick steps had me there, and I dropped my shoulder to catch his chest and knock him back. He let out a quiet puff of air as I hit him and collapsed into a crumpled heap in front of the door. I overbalanced—he had been lighter and more easily knocked aside than I had expected—and I landed awkwardly atop him. I clambered to my knees, and hunted through his pockets for the key, while everyone else in the room stood frozen in surprise. He wasn't moving.

Amy was the first to react, grabbing the poker from beside the fire and brandishing it in front of Mabel. "Do not move," she snarled. Goose-flesh prickled down my neck at the tone of her voice, I believe she would have struck the old woman if she had needed to. Fortunately, Mabel also believed her, and stayed in her seat. She craned her neck to see her husband, fear etched on her face.

I found the key, slotted it into the keyhole, and flung the front door wide. "Come on," I urged. The shock broke, Chambers gathered up his wife and their tearful children and they dashed out past me. "Careful!" I called after them. "The Martian might already be nearby."

Amy inched away from Mabel, aiming the poker at her the whole time. When she reached the fallen Arthur, she knelt and checked his pulse. "He's alive," she called out. "I suggest you tend to him, rather than pursuing us," she added. She then grabbed the key from the door, tugged me outside, and locked the door behind us.

Chambers and his wife were lifting their children into the rear of the cart as Amy and I caught up to them. Amy, still brandishing the poker, refused to take her eyes from the front door until we were sure that we were not being pursued. The smoke from the cottage chimney now had an unearthly green hue to it, doubtless this was the effect that curious log had imparted.

If the Martian had noticed the signal, he was still too far away for us to see him, and we had to hope that the reverse was still true. Chambers and I put our backs into hauling the cart away as quickly as possible, our wives pushing from the rear until we had to slow for fear of exhausting ourselves.

"We needn't fear pursuit from those two, at least," I mused. "Even pulling this cart, we're faster than they could ever be."

"They might show the Martians the route we took," Amy said. "If they do have some arrangement with them, we might yet find him on our tail."

"Nonsense," I said. "They were the mere delusions of people who had endured the unthinkable."

You sound almost sorry for them," Chambers said.

"I empathise with their loss, of course. I can feel pity even as I condemn their acts. The Martians do not recruit allies among humanity, do not communicate with us and do not spare anyone, no matter their usefulness."

"I was thinking about that," Chambers said. "Is it so impossible? The British Empire requires the help of local staff to operate, as did the Roman Empire in antiquity. It would simplify their operations if they could delegate to those who evolved on this planet. Not to mention reducing their frequency of contact with us, and all the risks that would entail."

I laughed at his idea. "They've never shown the slightest interest in us as sentient," I reminded him. "They wipe out most of us, and devour the rest." I saw Mary shuddering out of the corner of my eye and lowered my voice. "They have never attempted communication, and all our attempts have met with destruction." I remembered Ogilvy a lifetime ago, leading a contingent of men towards the first of the cylinders in Horsell, under a white flag.

"If they communicate directly from mind to mind, as we speculate, then they might attempt to contact us at every encounter. They might take our lack of response as evidence of hostility, even before we bring guns to bear on them."

"Even if telepathy between Martians is possible, we have no ability to employ it ourselves."

"What of mediums, mind-readers?" Chambers asked.

"Parlour tricks, or charlatans," I replied. "None has ever stood up to scientific scrutiny."

"It would only take one," he said. "One human who could do it, and if they had come across him, he could be their ambassador."

"Or her," Amy pointed out.

"Even if I allow for that possibility," I said, "those two showed no sign of magical abilities. All their actions were directed by self-preservation and their misguided beliefs, not evidence. They never suggested they had spoken to the Martians."

Now that the terror of our escape had passed, the lead was returning to my limbs. I stumbled over the loose earth and caught myself with the cart-trace. The tiredness came from nowhere, and with it regret at my actions. I had charged that old man with all my strength, uncaring whether I knocked him aside or shattered his bones. I noticed an ache in my shoulder where it had hit his solar plexus, and recalled with alarm his pale, unconscious face.

"Was he truly alive?" I whispered to Amy, terrified of her reply.

She nodded. "You had no choice, remember that," she said. "All of us were in danger, and you acted in the only way possible."

"He looked so pale," I said. "Are you sure?"

"Absolutely. His pulse was strong. If you did him any injury, it wasn't a threat to his life. Perhaps it will cause him to think again before trying the same trick with someone else."

We had no means to put up notices, so there was no way to warn any other travellers who might stumble this way. I hoped Amy was right, and that they would not try to entrap anyone further.

Dusk was encroaching, and we judged ourselves far enough from the cottage to risk bedding down for the night. We pulled the cart off the road through a farm gate and tucked under the canopy of a tree to better hide it from discovery. We spread our tarpaulin over the back, agreed the watch rota, and settled down to sleep.

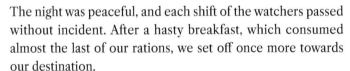

The night was peaceful, and each shift of the watchers passed without incident. After a hasty breakfast, which consumed almost the last of our rations, we set off once more towards our destination.

"We ought to reach our decision point today," Chambers noted casually. "Have we any further thoughts about our destination?"

"We have no additional information over the last time we discussed this," I said. "And so I fear we will be at the same impasse."

"We have enough food for one more decent meal," Chambers said. "So, if we head to Wiltshire and find it destroyed, we will be hungry on our retreat."

"You're quick to assume it will be abandoned," I said. "Even if it is, we might well rest and rebuild our supplies before continuing our mission."

"Then we shall vote," Amy declared. "All of us."

"Even the children?" Chambers asked. "They hardly have the knowledge required."

"True enough," Mary said. "I would not have them embark on a sea voyage, in any case. So I shall cast my vote for Wiltshire."

"Well, I vote for Bristol, and then to Canada," Chambers said, with an apologetic look at his wife. Anger flashed in her eyes for a moment, before being replaced with sadness. "We have lost enough time to this journey already, and should get under way as quickly as possible. And we still have no information on Wiltshire."

"I agree," Amy said. "Canada is our best path to continuing the fight, and we should head there as fast as we can."

All eyes turned to me. If I picked Canada, the vote was won, and the decision made. A vote for Wiltshire would leave us deadlocked once again. My mind raced. I didn't think it appropriate to drag the children to Canada and expose them to who knew what dangers. But leaving us undecided would delay us further, or even risk splitting us up. If it came to that, Amy and Chambers would head across the ocean, I was sure, while Mary would take the children to where she believed they would be safe. And what would I do? I wouldn't choose to leave Amy's side, but I could hardly send Mary on with her children unprotected, either.

There was no logical way out of this, so I had to vote with my heart and my beliefs. "I vote Wiltshire," I said. "My brother may be there still, and safety. And if it has fallen, we shall find supplies somewhere."

"So much for democracy," Amy said. "The impasse remains."

"Then how do we decide?" I asked. "Toss of a coin?"

"Perhaps the children's needs should be the deciding vote?" Mary suggested.

"Hush," Chambers said, earning another stern glance from his wife. "Look." He pointed up the road in front of us.

# Chapter Seven

# Rendezvous

At first I did not see what had alarmed him, so sure I was that he had seen a Martian that I scanned above the horizon before my eyes dropped back to the road ahead. Tucked under a tree at the crossroads was a tarpaulin, stretched taut to form a rudimentary tent.

"Someone has passed this way?" I said. "It is not surprising, given how many escaped the camp. And some must have made it past the traitors, I am sure."

"You assume it is one of ours, and not another sympathiser," Chambers hissed. "We should be on our guard."

We chocked the cart's wheels and left Amy and Mary with the children once more. Chambers grabbed a crowbar from the back, and I gathered the poker Amy had wielded. Should the need arise, these would need to do as weapons. Cautiously, we stalked along the hedges lining the road until we were within a few yards of the makeshift shelter.

"Hullo!" I called out and saw Chambers jump out of the corner of my eye. "Anyone there?"

"Bloody hell!" a familiar voice called out. A face appeared around the side of the canvas, and I almost dropped my weapon in surprise.

"Russell?" I cried. "What on earth are you doing here?"

"Counting my lucky stars you came along," he called back. "Come on, get off the road."

Chambers walked back to gather the cart while I walked over to Russell's camp. I found him sat on a grass-stained blanket, his leg wrapped and splinted, propped up on a nearby tree stump. I asked what happened.

"Stupid leg," he muttered. "Went out from under me as I climbed a gate, and my damned knee-cap dislocated. I almost passed out from the pain, my companions had to stuff a leather belt in my teeth to stop me crying out when they put it back in. But I couldn't walk, and it would only have slowed them down trying to carry me, so I urged them to go on ahead. They'll send rescue when they get to Wiltshire, shouldn't be long now."

Knowing Russell, it surprised me that he had the altruism required to send his fellow travellers away. Although if they'd abandoned him, I suspect he'd have no compunctions about telling us, so perhaps I was doing him a disservice.

"Well, we have a cart and can get you back under way," I said.

Chambers and the others had joined us. "Not if we're not heading that way," Chambers said. "We've yet to decide."

"We have a casting vote now," I pointed out, with a nod at Russell. Before Chambers could protest, I laid out the choices.

"It's obvious," Russell said. I braced myself, certain he would insist on heading to Canada. "Wiltshire is the only logical choice."

"Logical?" Chambers protested. "What logic could bring you to that conclusion?"

"Simple," Russell said. "If the government sanctuary has fallen, we'd have seen refugees by now. They knew of the plan to leave via Bristol, and this is the crossroads they'd come through. Why do you think I chose to camp here? For the view? We've seen no-one yet, ergo the site survives."

"And if they didn't get out?" Chambers asked.

"Then at least some of our own merry band of travellers would be coming back this way by now, having discovered that fact," Russell said smugly. "Or at worst, we'll run into them on our way. So, who'll give me a hand into your cart?"

As glad as I was that Russell had cast the deciding vote in my favour, it surprised me he was preaching caution. Perhaps his injury had made him more cautious, or maybe he just feared that the sailors we hoped to meet would refuse an injured man passage. In any case, Amy and Chambers accepted the democratic result, not to mention Russell's logical conclusion, with grace, and we set off united towards Wiltshire.

As we continued our journey, Mary filled Russell in on the trouble we had encountered.

"Ah," he laughed, "I wondered why you greeted your old friend with brandished arms! For a moment, I thought perhaps you had grown sick of me." I glanced over my shoulder to see Amy stifling a giggle with her hand and disguising it as a yawn. I turned back to hide my grin and caught Chambers rolling his eyes in mock exasperation. Of all the people we might have hoped to encounter *en route*, he would not have been our first choice, but I admit I was glad that he had suffered no greater injury than a sprained knee. Russell was probably the best mind we had among the many arrayed against the Martians, and we couldn't afford to lose him.

"I am not surprised to hear of your woes," he continued. "After all, I speculated about the possibility of sympathisers and traitors before the second invasion." I bit my tongue, remembering all too well the argument I had endured when he doubted the truth of my encounter with the religious fanatics at Horsell. And I didn't remind him of his surprise at the idea of a saboteur being involved in the destruction of the Ironclad *William Kite*. If he should feel the need to paint himself as the ultimate authority on every subject, it was worth allowing him to do so as the cost of a quiet life.

"How did you avoid them yourself?" I enquired innocently. "Did you and your colleagues not encounter them?"

Russell was helping himself to some of our provisions, and didn't reply until he had swallowed a mouthful of preserved meat. "I think we must have taken an alternative route, we were forced into a detour to avoid a Martian," he explained. "We saw no smoke, nor would we have been... impulsive enough to investigate if we had."

Being abandoned on the side of the road seemed to have mellowed him enough to call our actions 'impulsive' rather than what I believed he truly thought of such compassion. Sadly, a day or two without company had left him talkative, meaning that Amy and Mary found themselves on the receiving end of several lectures on Martian physiology and psychology, along with detailed descriptions of his work (or rather that of his scientists) on the bacteria he hoped would break through their defences.

The relentless drone of his pontificating spurred us to push a little harder, and before sunset we were approaching the hill which we believed overlooked the Wiltshire site and refuge.

"We've still not met anyone returning," Chambers said when we stopped for breath at the top of the hill. Even with Amy and Mary pushing the cart, the added weight of Russell combined with the lateness of the hour had winded us by the time we reached the summit. "Russell may be right that the site remains untroubled."

I wished for binoculars so that I might observe any comings and goings down in the valley. I had to console myself with the idea that any Martian activity would be visible, even from this distance. Nevertheless, we were all quiet on the long meandering descent, as though we might be overheard and ambushed at any moment.

After around a half a mile, we reached a section that formed a steeper descent. We paused to prepare ourselves and were just about to set off again when a voice called out.

"Halt!"

We froze in place, apart from Russell, who threw a blanket over his head and ducked down inside the cart. A soldier emerged from concealment on the side of the road, his rifle aimed directly at me. His eyes flicked between the adults arranged around the cart and then saw the children's faces peering curiously over the side.

"Who goes there?" he asked. We spoke over each other in our eagerness to introduce ourselves, and so it took a few moments for him to realise who we were. Once he understood we were additional refugees from Shropshire, he relaxed, and his gun barrel sank to point harmlessly at the floor.

At that moment, Russell evidently decided the danger had passed, and stuck his own head up over the side of the cart. This so startled the guard that he swung his rifle back up and fired without warning. Fortunately, his panic had affected his aim, and the round whistled harmlessly over Russell's head.

"What the devil do you think are you doing?" I would have expected that outburst to come from Russell, but he had ducked back into cover at the sound of the rifle-shot. Instead, it came from Mary, who was now charging towards her children. They were unharmed, if scared, and she comforted them before rounding on the soldier. He at least had the good sense to sling his rifle over his back and plead for forgiveness.

"I'm sorry, ma'am, he startled me, I thought he was about to attack!"

"I don't give a fig if he was a Martian," Mary bellowed, "if you so much as raise your voice towards my children, I will show you what an attack truly looks like!"

"Perhaps you can show us to the gate?" Chambers asked, a steel in his own voice I had not heard before. "Unless you wish to keep using us for target practice?"

The soldier gave us directions, waving his arm down the road, and we set off once again. His apologies followed us down the steep hill until he was out of earshot.

## Chapter Eight

# Wiltshire

A short distance down the slope another soldier directed us onto a spur road that wound around the hill, signposted for a quarrying works. We reached the gate a few minutes afterwards, which was guarded by two rather more professional soldiers. These men took our names and allowed us to pass without incident, although they instructed us to leave the cart just inside the gate. There was a small paddock with pit-ponies and horses grazing on sparse grass, and we pulled our worthy transport alongside a couple of similar vehicles parked nearby.

Each of us gathered his or her belongings from the back and followed directions to the entrance of the underground section a short distance away. Another pair of soldiers nodded a greeting to us, and we headed down into the mine.

The roof of the tunnel was not so low that we had to crawl, although Chambers and I were forced to hunch over to avoid banging our heads. Russell was just short enough to avoid injury, being bent over to the side as Chambers supported him under the arm. Amy and Mary could walk normally, and of course, the children were untroubled by the restricted space. They were not fond of the gloom, however, and needed some reassurance from their parents before they would proceed inside. Once there, the discovery of the echoes they could produce by shouting or clapping their hands delighted them.

We allowed them to indulge themselves for a while before asking for quiet. They obliged, and soon the only sound was the drip of water from some unseen source, and the muted padding of our feet as we made our way deeper into the hillside.

Lamps hung every few feet, casting small puddles of light around themselves, and these provided just enough illumination to see where we were going. The path underfoot was surprisingly smooth and even for a mine-works, but at one of the lamps Chambers noticed some evidence that a narrow-gauge railway had been recently removed.

"Look, here's a tie-down that would have secured the rails."

"I wish to goodness they'd left it," Russell complained, "It would save my knee to ride the railway in comfort."

"They probably needed the iron," Chambers said, who was shouldering most of Russell's weight. "And with not quarrying any longer, there was no need for regular carts."

"Be glad you're here at all," Mary muttered, "and weren't shot for your idiocy." I saw Russell open his mouth to retort before he thought better of it.

We trudged in silence for what must have been a quarter of a mile or so before the tunnel curved to the left. As we rounded the shallow bend, I noticed a dim glow in the distance, which grew brighter as we continued. Before long, we encountered a larger cavern, well illuminated and bustling with people. The ceiling here was almost seven feet, allowing us to stand up straight, and I eased out the cricks in my back. There were people seated at typical office desks, rummaging through filing cabinets and scurrying back and forth to book cases all over the space. The impression was exactly that of a typical government office, such as the one in which I had visited my brother before the invasion, when you disregarded the rough-hewn rock walls in place of wood panels and wainscoting. Someone had even procured a large rug, which was so dusty now as to obscure whatever pattern had previously adorned it.

Chambers lowered Russell into a chair and stretched his own back out with a grunt. "Right," he said, "now what?"

I looked around myself again with more purpose. At the nearest desk, the one with the rug in front, sat a young woman who I took to be a receptionist. I strode over and introduced myself and my fellow travellers.

"Shropshire?" she enquired. When I nodded, she retrieved a manilla folder and extracted a few sheets from inside. "Those names again, please?"

As I reeled off our names, she ticked them off on her list. When I finished, she smiled at me and bade us welcome. "We shall arrange accommodation for you all, of course, and if you have any friends or family here already, then we'll ensure you're reunited. We have a handful of people from Shropshire here already, and most are in C-Wing." She tapped a small bell on her desk and the chamber echoed with the high-pitched ringing. Everyone glanced over, and one man came over to meet us.

"Fresh meat, Jennie?" he laughed, and then introduced himself. "Richard Adler, at your service. Let's find you some beds, shall we?"

I hesitated and turned back to Jennie. "My brother," I said. "I believe he was here?"

She pulled another folder from her desk drawer and flicked through the pages within, muttering his name under her breath. "Ah yes, I'll have him informed. Look after them, Dick," she called to our guide.

Adler beckoned us to follow him and led us towards another narrow tunnel with a whitewashed letter 'C' painted above it. This tunnel was high enough for us to continue walking

upright, although it echoed with sharp and loud metallic noises. These became louder the deeper we went until at one
point Adler stopped. He pulled a whistle from his pocket and
gave it a long, shrill blast. My ears rang long after the echoes
stopped, and I was about to remonstrate with him when I
realised the other sounds had ceased. He ushered us onwards,
and we came across a pair of men with picks, shovels and
a wheelbarrow who had evidently just stopped working on
the tunnel. They were shirtless, drenched in sweat, and stood
aside to let us pass. From that point on, the tunnel was only
about five feet high, and the adults all had to proceed in a
comical bent-legged walk, which made supporting Russell all
the harder. Thankfully, only a few hundred yards remained,
and we could unfurl ourselves into another atrium.

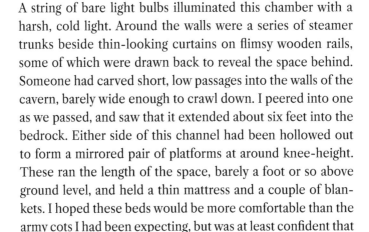

A string of bare light bulbs illuminated this chamber with a
harsh, cold light. Around the walls were a series of steamer
trunks beside thin-looking curtains on flimsy wooden rails,
some of which were drawn back to reveal the space behind.
Someone had carved short, low passages into the walls of the
cavern, barely wide enough to crawl down. I peered into one
as we passed, and saw that it extended about six feet into the
bedrock. Either side of this channel had been hollowed out
to form a mirrored pair of platforms at around knee-height.
These ran the length of the space, barely a foot or so above
ground level, and held a thin mattress and a couple of blankets. I hoped these beds would be more comfortable than the
army cots I had been expecting, but was at least confident that
they would be softer than the straw-lined cart we had spent
our past few nights in.

The room was all but empty, although I suppose there might have been people sleeping behind the closed curtains. I doubted they would be, however, as once the workmen in the tunnel resumed their work, the echoes of their tools would have rendered sleep impossible.

"At what time do they finish?" Amy asked.

"Usually at dinner-time," Adler replied. "That should let the kiddies get some rest."

Our host showed us our rooms, if we could describe them as such. Amy and I had a pair of beds to ourselves, and a shared trunk outside the curtain in which we could place our few belongings. Chambers and his family had two bedrooms assigned, something I later learned was not common. Most families had to make do with their children lying on mat-tresses placed on the floor between their beds, or share the beds themselves, which was precarious given they were very narrow. Because of his importance, Chambers and his family could choose whether to occupy one room with his wife, and deposit the children next door, or take a child each. They elected to try the former, and hope that nightmares would not plague the children.

There was no light inside our bedroom, and I made a mental note to ask for a lantern to use later on, should I wish to write before going to sleep. When I pulled the curtain closed across the entrance, however, I realised it was far too thin to block any light, and the movement of people outside cast eerie shadows over us as we took stock of our surroundings.

The low ceiling over the beds made sitting up impossible, and so Amy and I lay down for a few moments to test the comfort and gather our thoughts. Our mattress, while thin, seemed serviceable, and even though the pillow provided was under-stuffed, it would certainly be a decent place to sleep. The temperature was cool, but comfortable, and I suspected that it never varied this deep underground, no matter the weather on the surface. With winter approaching, that was a comforting thought. The air wasn't what I would describe as fragrant, but neither was it stale. The miners who had originally quarried this cavern had evidently taken measures to ensure a supply of fresh air while they worked, and we reaped the benefit of their hard labour now.

Despite our tiredness, there was no danger of falling asleep with the racket from the tunnel, and so we set off back to the main chamber in search of information. I was keen to see my brother again, while Chambers and Amy both wished to make progress on their plan towards visiting Canada. Mary said she would seek other families with children so that theirs might have some playmates, and see whether there was anything to keep them entertained. Russell wanted to join us, but we insisted on depositing him at the infirmary to have his leg examined.

"If they say you can join us," Amy told him, "then we will come and get you. Otherwise, follow their instructions."

"But I must be involved in the preparations," he protested. "The trip to Canada, the research, all of it. So few of us survived, I think I can say without bragging that I am the country's leading expert on almost all matters scientific. Not that I might not have been before, of course."

"If you make that knee worse," Amy said, "then you'll be no use to anyone. Your scientists can manage without you for a day or two, and so can we. And we can't be taking an invalid to Canada with us, so you'd better rest up."

Russell at least knew when he was beaten and submitted to the doctor's examinations with only minimal grumbling. The doctor was pleased for the activity, the infirmary having no other occupants. I had expected injured refugees from our own camp, but realised with a sinking heart that anyone who hadn't escaped alongside us would be dead and gone, not merely wounded.

Leaving Russell to the doctor's over-eager ministrations, the rest of us headed off to our various appointments. Amy and Chambers set off for the planning offices, and I promised to meet them as soon as possible. Someone informed Mary that they had set a small schooling area up in A-Wing, something that thrilled her and dismayed the children in equal measure. She dragged the protesting youths off and wished the rest of us good luck.

I arrived at the main entrance and peered around, looking for my brother. People were still milling about, coming and going from narrow tunnels with clipboards and papers to replenish the piles on the desks whenever they threatened to dip too low. I did not know what could be so vital, and so in need of documentation, as to occupy so many people amid such destruction.

"Remarkable, don't you think?"

I recognised my brother's voice immediately and spun around to greet him. My heart leapt to my mouth when I saw his face.

A long, ragged scar, now healed but still angry-looking, marred his right cheek. It extended up beneath his greying hairline, crossing his eye, which was a mere black orb in its socket. I realised with a start that he had replaced it with a glass one, or at least some stand-in for one.

"Ah, so it's noticeable then?" he asked. He was utterly serious for a moment, long enough for me to wonder if this place had no mirrors, before he burst into laughter, his face wrinkling with joy except for the stiffened area around the scar. "Don't worry," he chuckled, "it's not as bad as it looks." He leaned in closer and lowered his voice slightly. "And the ladies seem to approve, they say it makes me look heroic."

"How... how did it happen?" I asked.

"Would you believe in single, unarmed combat with a Martian? Face to face, or what passes for one in his case."

"Truly?" I gasped.

He laughed again. "No, nothing so exciting. A bit of mining equipment broke, and the drill-heads shattered." He turned serious. "I was one of the luckier ones, if I'm honest."

## Chapter Nine

# Brother

I had a thousand questions for him, had rehearsed so many of them in my mind on the journey, but now that the opportunity had arrived I found myself tongue-tied. His injury reminded me he had experienced his own adventures, and that I might never comprehend them all. We regarded each other seriously for a moment until the tension broke and we laughed together for the first time in years.

"How much we have done, and how little it matters now," he said, when the amusement passed. "We are here, and we are alive, and we are the lucky ones."

"I feared the worst when we lost contact with you," I said. "And then our own base being destroyed so easily..."

"The Martians seemed able to block our communications," he agreed. "But we didn't consider that their transmissions implied they could also listen to us."

I gasped. "They've been eavesdropping on us?"

"No," he laughed, "not what we say. At least, we don't believe they can understand us. They can determine that we're talking to one another and triangulate our position. When the first remote site went silent, we assumed they had been discovered by patrolling Martians. Much as your base was, they were all above ground, of course, and could hardly be hidden."

"We had warned them off with the heat-ray," I said. "And the blast of our Ironclad certainly soured them on exploring again, too. Perhaps they thought we were a bigger threat than we were. We didn't see one between that fight and the eventual destruction."

"So it took us a while to realise that they were using our own transmissions against us. It was only when we saw increased numbers searching the hills here that we suspected. We sent out runners with field radios to warn the camps, but their range was limited compared to the main antenna here." He shook his head. "I argued to send one last message from here, ordering radio silence, but I was overruled. Our survival was deemed more important."

"They well knew our location," I said. "And I suspect the same was true all over. A warning would not have bought us any safety."

"You're kind to say it, but the decision still haunts me."

Over the first decent cup of tea I had enjoyed in weeks, I filled him in on the details of our journey. He hung on my every word, which, of course, flattered my pride as a storyteller. When I came to the elderly couple who would have handed us over to the Martians, he called over one of the army men scurrying about, and had me describe the location.

"Check into that cottage," he ordered the man, "but do not harm the residents. These circumstances try all our strengths and I will not have them punished without a fair trial." The man saluted, and ran off, presumably to gather a small party. "It should not surprise me you bear them no ill will," my brother continued, "you were always understanding of the lengths men may go to in dire circumstances. Ever since your own experiences, the last time..."

I nodded, not trusting myself to speak for a moment.

He gave a watery smile. "We'll treat them fairly, despite their crimes."

"You have the authority to decide that? I suspect the government will be keen to make an example of them, hang them as traitors."

"The government comprises a few junior ministers who are rapidly realising they are out of their depth, and a slightly larger contingent of civil servants, such as myself." He tipped an imaginary hat to me. "We do most of the actual work, while the politicians meet endlessly about policies for regeneration."

"Regeneration? They're planning new towns while we cower in the dark?" I could scarcely believe what I was hearing.

"Someone"—at this word a familiar glint crept into his eye—"may have suggested that normal election cycles would be disrupted for a while, and so they should look at things on a longer timescale than they were accustomed to. It keeps them out of trouble and limits the damage they can cause."

"So you have effected a coup?" I asked in a whisper, looking around myself. "Usurped the democratically elected government?"

"Technically speaking, yes. But they can call an election any time, should they so wish. We have a precise census of survivors to create the most accurate electoral roll ever seen. However, they know they are viewed with a great deal of mistrust by the general population for their perceived failings, and indeed are blamed for the entire fall of humanity, so they have little incentive to do so."

"I am surprised that someone has not strung them up themselves, or cast them out to face the world they have created," I said.

"That's not really the British way," my brother chuckled. "We're much more satisfied muttering under our breath and tutting quietly, than fomenting revolution."

I stared at him incredulously.

"I jest," he said. "The people here have seen enough destruction and death to last a dozen lifetimes, and would much rather avoid inflicting it on others. And most were civil servants before the fall, and are perfectly happy with the status quo. Forcing a transfer of power would mean becoming accountable for their own actions, and few have the stomach for it."

"So apart from running what remains of the country," I asked Frederick, "what occupies your time here?"

He sighed. "I made a rod for my own back. When I stepped in to form some sort of order, it cemented me as the 'go-to' man for any crisis, problem, or complaint."

"You always were capable in a pinch," I admitted. "But even so, I didn't have you pegged as the type to be a leader. I mean no offence," I added, "I merely did not think such a position would have appealed to you."

"It did not. But you must understand what those early days were like. We had this place running with a skeleton staff, awaiting the arrival of the government and the selected few who would join them. Everything we had prepared for the past year assumed we would be supporting the continuity of rule, acting to fulfil the desires of those who had been chosen to lead. When barely a handful of them made it here in time, and," he lowered his voice and glanced around, "mostly the junior ones, still wet behind the ears, it rather cast our preparations into disarray."

"I just assumed it would be a well-oiled machine, like our refuge in Shropshire," I said.

"That was an existing army base, with a well-defined purpose and a leadership in situ. Your and Amy's arrival was neither expected nor necessary, and so the place continued on, unperturbed."

His dismissal of my necessity stung me. "I feel I have contributed a great deal," I huffed. "If nothing else, I have delivered both Russell and Chambers to you—still on speaking terms, no less—when without my 'unanticipated arrival', that was not a foregone conclusion."

Frederick laughed and placed his hand on my shoulder. "I meant only that the base was a going concern without you, not that you had no purpose. But you rather prove my point about making ourselves indispensable. Chambers and Russell, I suspect, now cannot even decide what to have for dinner without checking with you first, hmm?"

"Of course they can," I retorted, and then recalled the last of their discussions in which they had forced me to intervene. Only that last morning in Shropshire I had resolved an argument over office supplies. "Though I admit they might come to blows over the distribution of paper-clips." I smiled at a mental image of the pair of them flinging stationary at one another from behind upturned desks.

"There you are. Once you solve one problem, you become indispensable. And so it is with me now. I brought forth order from chaos, and my reward is yet more chaos to wrangle. I should much prefer to take a brief holiday to Canada with you, and settle disagreements about luncheon meat."

"You won't be going?" I gasped. "I just assumed..."

"I rather hoped you might step into my shoes," he replied. The scar crinkled as he smiled.

"Me? I'm no diplomat!"

"I rather think you will have to be," he said. "Russell has become a very capable scientist, and though I hate to admit it, he's also one of our senior soldiers now. Though he lacks enough of an army these days to do much soldiering. Even Amy has grown into her new role, from what I've heard. We are all required to wear several hats these days."

"I can't be your only option," I protested.

"No. But I believe you are the best one."

During our time in the cart, Russell had once again expounded on the benefits of his research project into bacteria and viruses that could defeat the Martian defences. He was convinced that this was the only way to ensure a victory, and to send a message that any future invasion attempts would be repelled as the last one had.

Chambers, of course, still favoured more direct action, using his idea of atomic weapons to disrupt the machinery that the invaders relied upon. Each had spent a lot of energy to convince me that his was the only correct path, but I wasn't sure that either had the potential for victory alone.

My brother shared my opinion. "I doubt there are enough of us left to take the fight to the Martians in any meaningful way, so Chambers' device will only be useful in a narrow, tactical manner. If we are to see the Martians off, Russell's approach offers us the best chance, but it's a gamble whether he can devise an infection that will do the trick."

"He seems sure that he can," I said. "And his discovery of that anti-bacterial compound might let us test against their defences before we release it. If we can get it to spread without the Martians realising, they might not have time to develop a counter-measure."

"He's on the absolute fringe of what we understand about biology," my brother pointed out. "A breakthrough might be days away, or years. We'd be fools to put all our eggs in one basket."

"So we pursue both?" I asked. A wave of tension that I had not noticed that I was holding left my body. I realised I had feared having to argue with Frederick over the correct approach, and convince him that once again a compromise would have to be reached. Fortunately, he had already assessed the situation in the same way as I had. Now it only remained to convince Russell and Chambers.

"I doubt either of them will be delighted with that," Frederick laughed.

# Chapter Ten

# Scheme

As predicted, both men thought us fools for pursuing the ideas of the other, rather than throwing our entire efforts behind their own plan. I was glad of my brother's support to calm them down, though I think by now both were used to my habit of finding the centre ground between their proposals.

One slight advantage we had was Russell's relative immobility. He was in no state to travel, and the doctors had prescribed bed rest for at least a fortnight, followed by a month or more of rehabilitation and monitoring before he might be back to his usual agility. Naturally, he refuted this.

"I shall be fine in no time," he argued. "A few days in the cart to Bristol and a leisurely sea voyage will do me the world of good you'll see."

"That would barely take us to two weeks," I said, "and that's assuming we even take the cart this time. It slowed us down, after all."

"They have animals here, there were horses at the entrance."

"And you're assuming that the ship's crew would take you aboard at anything less than fighting fitness," Chambers said. "They will need all hands to work the ship, I expect, and would expect any passengers to pull their weight."

"Quite likely," my brother piped up.

"You've been in contact with them, then?" I asked.

"Just before your arrival," he replied. "We sent runners out to radio them from the high ground, and they're offshore as we speak. They are shorthanded, as you surmised, many of the crew wished to set off in search of their families when they returned."

"What luck there is a ship at all," Amy said. "Were they at sea when the invasion happened?"

"There were a few that were out of reach of land when the Martians arrived," my brother explained. "This vessel, the Minadora, spotted the black smoke rolling into the sea as they approached shore, and the captain wisely pulled back over the horizon. When no replies came to his radio calls, he assumed the worst. Eventually he came into contact with us, and we coordinated sending the crew ashore when it was safe. Now they keep a safe distance, and we resupply them from time to time."

"What makes a safe distance?" Russell asked. "Remember, they sank the Thunderchild at sea."

"I was there," my brother reminded him. "And that was in shallow water, almost as close to shore as the vessel could get. Not to mention, she was covering the evacuations and taking a greater risk in order to preserve lives. The Martians lack any means of navigating the water, there not being oceans on Mars. So they are limited to the length of their tripod's legs. Even with the larger models we have encountered, they cannot pass more than a mile or so into the Bristol Channel."

Amy could no longer contain herself. "Enough talk, when are we to depart?"

I stifled a smile.

"The day after tomorrow," my brother said. "Preparations were under way before your arrival, and I see no need to delay any further."

Russell raised a hand in protest. "We have not yet decided my role."

"We have," my brother replied. "You are to oversee the biological research here, as the best use of your remarkable talents. I would not waste a mind such as yours on a mere 'fetch and carry' operation, even if you were at full fitness." That familiar glint was back in his eye, and I struggled to maintain my straight face. Amy didn't even try, but Russell did not notice, and took my brother's words at face value.

"Well, I'm sure I can improve efficiencies for you, direct the research away from any dead ends. If you are sure, that is?"

"Quite sure," my brother replied, and with a last smile at us all, left the room.

The next two days passed painfully slowly. Amy and I had little enough to prepare, as what meagre belongings we had rescued from Woking had been destroyed along with the camp. We were issued a couple of changes of clothing and such necessities as the base had to spare, chiefly toiletries.

The preparations prior to the invasion had been thorough; the food was plentiful and decent, someone had ensured that there was a hefty supply of tea available, and we enjoyed what might prove to be our last few hours of creature comforts for quite some time. I read a little, though the base's supply of books was uneven. Most of the volumes were non-fiction in nature, being guides to technology and machinery that some erstwhile civil servant had deemed vital to rebuilding the world in the event of a catastrophe. While I could not argue with his logic, I wished he had been more of a patron of the arts and had included more than a token collection of fictional works.

"The British Library was charged with protecting as much of literature as could be saved," my brother informed me. "In vaults across the country, they were storing the finest works, although I'm not sure how many they have actually preserved."

"Perhaps the building itself remains," I said, "and the works inside."

"Perhaps. But we had to assume that it would not, and plan accordingly. Likewise for the National Gallery, and the major museums. Most have storage locations outside the capital, and hopefully transferred their major works and collections there for safe keeping."

"At least we shall not be starting from scratch," I said. "I had feared a new dark age, with only what we remembered from before to guide us."

"It will still not be easy," my brother pointed out. "We built much of civilisation upon what came before, after all. We shall not be creating new steam engines without the machinery to build them, nor printing presses, clocks or any of a thousand other items. The Martians have set us back decades, if not a century."

"But much of that equipment might also survive," I said. "The Martians won't have need of it, and we saw no signs of their destroying things wantonly."

"You believe they will pass up a source of refined metals if they come across it? I expect they have ransacked every factory and industrial site in the world already to create raw materials for their machinery. We shall have to build up our technology once again, from the simplest building blocks."

"Restart the industrial revolution?" I despaired. "Will we really have to go back that far?"

"More or less," he said. "Of course, we can rely on our documents and experience to guide us. What took a century might be done in fifty years or even less, if we are lucky. But I do not believe the knowledge is what will hinder us."

"What then?" I asked. "When we win this war, we shall have the run of the Earth once more. And the technology of the Martians to pillage once more, why I shall be surprised if we do not leap-frog our previous achievements!"

"And who will do that? You forget, brother, that we have lost so many of our fellow men and women. The survivors here are capable, exceptional even, but there are precious few. The same has been repeated around the world, humanity is barely a shadow of its former self. With only a handful of scientists, where do you direct their research? With only a half-dozen engineers, what is their priority? Steam engines? Repairing sewers to avoid disease? Weapons of war, should our neighbours turn against us and covet what we are rebuilding?"

This last suggestion caught me utterly off-guard. "You cannot believe that nations will still war with one another, after this?" I gasped. "Are we not united in a common goal?"

"Right now, we might be," he said. "But you witnessed how the nations of the world reacted when we kept our knowledge of the Martian technology to ourselves. Imagine what they would do if we were the first to rebuild something they themselves needed."

"Why, we would share it, though, wouldn't we?"

"Would we? I agree that would be noble, but if we're struggling to feed ourselves, do you think the hungry man would volunteer to share his scraps with the starving across the ocean? When in history has mankind not put his own interests above that of his fellows?"

"I flatter myself that I am less sceptical about our basic decency," I said. "And the mere idea of nations seems ridiculous now, when we have all been reduced so much. The Martians are a common enemy right now, but when they are gone, do you not believe we can unite for a common purpose?"

"When men lack everything else, they resort to nationalism. We have encountered it repeatedly, a charismatic leader gains power by blaming the 'other' for all the problems of the population to stoke up hatred. What better means to spur men on than protecting your homeland? At present, the Martians fill that role, but who will be their replacement when they're gone? And what might we lose in the process?"

Chapter Eleven

# Departure

Such pessimism would have been hard to stomach from anyone else, but to hear such words from my brother was unimaginable. He had always been the most positive sort, keen to see the tiniest glimmer of light in the darkness. If he truly held such a gloomy view of our future, then it had to be considered. His position in government would have allowed him a view of the bigger picture that I lacked, and it forced me to consider his words an accurate prediction, no matter how little I cared for the idea.

During the last day before our departure, I watched the workings of the base with a newfound perspective. The men and women dashing around were less focused on the battles at hand than I had assumed, indeed most of the occupants of the shelter had never even seen a Martian war machine. Instead, they directed most of their activity towards preserving such knowledge and expertise as could be documented. These people were building a time-capsule of our society and ingenuity for future ages, so that when mankind once again mastered machinery, our descendants would have a guidebook to follow. My brother's goal was to avoid our descendants having to reinvent the wheel, in an almost literal sense.

The night before our voyage was due to start, Amy and I sat down in the dining area for a last meal in relative comfort. While the cave and its benched seating were hardly the salon at the Ritz, it would be markedly better than the conditions we could expect aboard the ship.

"Such a shame it could not have been the *Lusitania*," Amy sighed, "and we might have voyaged in luxury."

"There has been no word from her since the invasion, I understand." Immediately after the Martian invasion my brother had charged the radio operators with cataloguing all contact with ships. For a while there had been a plan to evacuate as many people as possible to floating refuges, where they would be safely out of reach of the invading forces. There had been no time to enact such a plan, the overwhelming speed of our conquest rendering any such ideas irrelevant. "Nor most of the other liners. Whether sunk or sheltering elsewhere, we shall have to make do with the Minadora."

"I know it was wishful thinking, of course. But I wonder why none of the liners seem to have returned."

"They would not have had supplies for more than their planned voyage, and with so many souls aboard, they would have had no choice but to put into port as planned. The merchantmen with smaller crews could have rationed supplies or even dug into their cargo to supplement their food supply. Imagine the outcry if they had asked first-class passengers to nibble on hard ships' biscuits or feast on rats from the hold!"

Amy shuddered. "I trust it will not come to that!"

"I am assured the Minadora has a full stock of food, at least slightly more palatable than that. Mostly dried and salted goods, along with some tinned items. We are, of course, supplementing their supplies as payment for their service, and providing for our own needs as best we can."

As we finished our meal, Chambers and Mary arrived in the dining area and took seats beside us.

"All set for the morning?" Chambers asked cheerfully. Mary sat quietly, unable to meet our eyes.

"Indeed," I replied. "It shall feel good to have a purpose again. Even a couple of days without direction has me quite restless. And yourself?"

He thought for a moment. "I confess I am in two minds," he said. "I need to do my part, of course, and I am the logical choice for the liaison with the scientists in Canada." He glanced over at his wife and took her hand. "But a significant part of me doesn't wish to leave my family. We have not been parted since this all began, and to head off into uncertain territory..." He and Mary exchanged an adoring look.

"Then stay," Amy said. After a moment, she laughed, quickly covering her mouth with her hand. "I am sorry, but you should see your faces," she added. "Like three goldfish out of water!" She opened her mouth into a circle and widened her eyes before giggling again.

"I cannot," Chambers began. "I must... I need to..."

Amy raised her eyebrows. "What must you do?" she asked. "As I understand it, we are merely errand boys after all, so do we need a scientist dogging our every step?"

"There might be questions," I said. "Issues with the ore which require a scientific understanding. Perhaps a situation or problem which we would not realise was even a concern, which Chambers would immediately spot."

"Is that true?" Amy asked.

Chambers reluctantly nodded.

"Then your path is clear, is it not?" Amy said.

"Why are you going?" Mary asked Amy in a quiet voice.

"There is nothing for me to do here," Amy replied. "The infirmary is empty, and besides, I decided in Shropshire that I would rather take action than follow the direction of fate. But you have your children," she added. "They are the future, and the most valuable things on this earth now. And so your calling is the highest one, to nurture and care for them."

"And is it not their father's role, also?" Chambers asked.

Once again, Amy did not hesitate. "Of course. But if he can do his part to ensure there is a world for them to inherit, then I, for one, believe he has a duty to do so."

We all sat in silence for a few minutes, considering Amy's words. Again I marvelled at her intelligence and her succinct grasp of the situation. I had barely considered the implications of Chambers' not joining us, and she had already talked him back into going.

"But perhaps the decision should not be yours," Amy added. "Or at least, not yours alone. Mary?"

All eyes turned to Chambers' wife, who shrank back under the attention. "I shall miss you," she said eventually, with a squeeze of his hand.

---

The journey to Bristol was not arduous, being a little over thirty miles and mostly downhill, but we were glad of the horses drawing the carts. We were bringing additional supplies for the sailors who, while availing themselves of the preserved items in their hold, had need of fresher produce. Scurvy, long since eradicated in our vessels at sea, was now a danger once more.

Those items, along with our own provisions for the trip to the docks, were too much of a load for a single cart. Split between two, however, they left ample room in each for passengers. We took turns to ride and rest our legs, and only on the steepest of inclines did we all have to get out and relieve the horses. In fact, we could spend almost half our time riding, and the horses could progress much quicker than Chambers and I had managed on our own journey.

Our team was ten in number, with Amy as the only woman. Chambers had expressed his fears privately to me that her presence might encourage some of the other wives to push for inclusion, but this had not happened. I wondered if he had urged the men to dissuade them, or whether the idea of a long sea voyage and uncertain perils had been enough to encourage them to remain at the base. In either case, Amy's presence was tolerated well enough, and her cooking won over any men who might have been perturbed on the first night. After a hearty stew and fresh-baked bread we had brought from the base, she confided in me she had planned this meal for that very purpose.

"I thought I would face more resistance," she whispered as we lay in our tent. "But what man can refuse a decent meal, even if I must play the role of dutiful housewife once more?"

"Not I," I agreed. "And I confess I have missed your cooking. But I know better than to force you into that role when there are more valuable uses of your time. I do hope, however, that this is not the last feast you will prepare?"

There was just enough moonlight filtering through the canvas to see her smile.

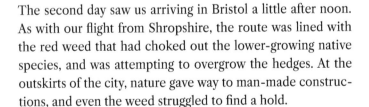

The second day saw us arriving in Bristol a little after noon. As with our flight from Shropshire, the route was lined with the red weed that had choked out the lower-growing native species, and was attempting to overgrow the hedges. At the outskirts of the city, nature gave way to man-made constructions, and even the weed struggled to find a hold.

Nevertheless, every crack in the concrete sprouted some, and where buildings had been destroyed in the fighting, the ruins were overgrown already. I thought I had grown used to the strong, metallic smell of the invasive plant, but in such narrow streets the scent built up to be sickening. As we approached the centre, the buildings were more intact; no doubt the residents had fled from here and put up little resistance, leaving that to the army further out. The weed buried the once-beautiful greens and parks of the city, and even clogged the river. We passed by the station, and I recalled with a shudder the brief halt we had made here during our evacuation. Crowds had been hammering at the gates, desperate to board a train out to some safe haven, while a military guard had ushered us through to somewhere that had offered us refuge for a while at least. The vast steel gates still chained shut across the entrance were bent and bowed, but had withstood the full terror of a city's people. I gave thanks for the sturdiness of Victorian engineering and returned my eyes to the road ahead.

We had seen no Martians on our short journey, and I wondered aloud at the idea. Chambers had also noticed, but it fell upon Lovett, our guide, to explain why.

"There's no people left to round up," he said glumly. "In the early days, we could barely leave the camp without spotting them prowling about, snatching up folks left and right. After a week we might only see one a day, and by the time you arrived it'd been almost a week since we last sighted one."

"I wish the same had been true for us," Amy said. "They seemed to have a particular interest in our camp."

"Probably the heat-ray," Chambers said, without thinking.

"How do you mean?" Lovett asked.

"The scientists were experimenting with one," I said, to cover Chambers' embarrassment. "It had been salvaged from the first invasion; our camp was a research station before the war."

"Did it work?"

"Not well enough," Amy said, "or we'd still be there."

"I wish we'd had one," Lovett mused. "Those early days were tense, I can tell you. We were trying to gather as much food as we could, you see, knowing the red weed was coming. And we had survivors showing up too, that we wanted to protect. If we'd been able to see the Martians off, even for a while, it might have made a difference." He shook his head sadly.

"You lost friends?" Amy asked him quietly.

He nodded.

"I'm sorry," she said. "But if you'd made yourselves a target, it could have been so much worse. By the latest reckoning, only a dozen made it out of our camp to get here."

"I guess so," he said with a sniff. "And I doubt there's any of us alive hasn't lost friends or family. We just have to get on with it, don't we?" He spurred the horses to speed up, and we rattled through the deserted city without another word.

# Chapter Twelve

# Purpose

I found the docks at Portishead eerie, and for the longest time, I couldn't figure out why. The cranes loomed overhead, cargo boxes and pallets were scattered around the place seemingly at random, but nothing looked out of the ordinary at all. Even the red weed was conspicuous by its absence. "Something to do with the sea air, salt doesn't agree with it," Lovett explained. It wasn't until we had settled down to lunch that I realised what was disturbing me.

"It's abandoned," I said, and then realised how stupid that sounded. "I mean, there's no damage, no sign of fighting, not even a broken box or dropped tool. It's as if everyone just decided not to come in to work that day, and the place has been frozen ever since."

"I believe that's precisely what happened," Chambers said. "We knew the cylinders were going to open up eventually, and your brother radioed whatever ships he could to stay at sea until the situation was clearer. So with nothing to do, the dock workers stayed home, or fled for the countryside, I suppose."

Once we had all eaten, Lovett ordered his radio operator to contact our vessel. The young lad tasked with hauling the radio around had to head off at least a mile to avoid giving away our correct location and intentions, should any Martian be monitoring the airwaves. He set off with a spring in his step that I could never have managed, burdened as he was, and headed along the coastline to a suitable spot.

While he was gone, we busied ourselves with investigating the cargo around us. We had found nothing of particular use apart from a consignment of machine parts. We carefully re-wrapped these in their oiled cloth and secured them into their chest. Lovett painted a symbol on the side to identify it as valuable and told me someone would collect it at some future time to help in the rebuilding process. We had worked up quite a sweat wielding crowbars and hammers by the time the radio-man returned, and were glad of the break while he gave his report.

The ship had replied; they were still in position over the horizon, and would send their boat to collect us at dusk. We were warned that it would take two trips. Unanimously the men decided that Amy would have to go on the first trip, and that as her husband I could join her. My protests at my special treatment were half-hearted as I was glad that Amy would be the first to safety. I had no wish to be parted from her again, even for so short a time as it might take to reach the ship. The rest cast lots to decide who would go in which order.

Chambers was also lucky in the draw, and would join us along with two others. We passed the time checking and rechecking our bags to ensure that nothing would fall out during the transfer to the boat. The Bristol Channel was not particularly exposed to the weather, so we had little worry about rough water at this end of our trip, but the transfer to the ship at sea might well prove more fraught. I advised Amy to change into trousers for the expedition, rather than her comfortable skirts. While she had owned some before, the difficulty of riding a bicycle in skirts making them necessary, they had not made it with us this far in our travels. Thus, she had planned ahead and borrowed some from a man at the base who most closely mirrored her physique, and repaired to one of the port buildings to change in privacy. She returned in a few minutes, and begged me for a belt, the waistband proving more generous than she had expected. A few moments later, she was ready for the voyage.

———————◄O►———————

Dusk fell, and we lit a single lantern, positioning it on the end of the jetty and pointing its beam out to sea. Chambers used a compass to align it to the expected heading of the boat, to aid them in their navigation. A fire or other signal might have been easier to use, but the risk of attracting attention from men or Martians was too great to consider. We took turns watching the horizon until the thin dark line between black ocean and grey sky blurred in front of our eyes, and the next man took over.

Lovett let out a cry after about an hour of waiting. "A light!" We all scurried to his side, and I confess I saw nothing for a few moments. Then a blink of yellowish light, easy to miss, and two more before a pause. Then three flashes again, a pause, and the cycle repeated. Lovett flashed our own lantern in response, and the first group gathered their belongings and supplies.

The boat drew up alongside, and it startled me to see how small it was. Two men sat on a plank fixed amidships, wielding an oar apiece, while another stood in the stern, operating the tiller. The boat was empty otherwise; not even a bench or plank for us to sit upon. They tied it to the jetty, and it bobbed gently up and down on the waves.

"Come along," the man at the tiller called in a whisper. "Pass your bags aboard first, then one by one we'll get you in."

"And where do we sit?" I asked.

"On your bag, on the floor, I don't much care," he replied. "I wouldn't sit on the side, though."

We passed our luggage over one bag at a time, and the three men deftly placed it in the boat's bottom. They carefully weighed each piece in their hands before assigning it a spot, and the boat itself remained perfectly level throughout. Clearly they were well-practised, and my confidence in their abilities outweighed my trepidation at setting to sea in a vessel I should not have been surprised to see on a boating lake in the summer.

Amy went aboard first, clambering elegantly over the side of the boat and only gently resting her hand on the arm of the nearest man top steady herself for a moment before arranging herself neatly at the bow. I went next, much less gracefully. My trouser leg caught on the rowlock, and only the strong and speedy intervention of the oarsmen prevented me from tumbling. I gasped my thanks, and made my way to sit beside Amy, almost crawling for fear of upsetting the boat or falling overboard.

"So my husband is no more a sailor than a soldier," she whispered, but without malice. I looked around, but the sailors were occupied with helping Chambers aboard and gave no signs of having overheard her comment. With no further mishap, everyone from the first batch was aboard, and they cast the ropes off.

A push from one oar sent us out into the Channel, where the current was faster. The men at the oars set up an easy rhythm, one they could sustain for hours if needed, but the flow of the river meant that the banks dashed past us, widening as we went, and before long I had lost sight of the land on either side in the dark.

Clouds had hung low all evening, and they still showed no sign of breaking up. The moon was only visible as a dull glow in a sector of the sky, but this and the compass were enough for our boatmen to navigate by. The boat barely rocked at first, and the quiet splash of the oars and gentle motion were extremely restful. My anxiety at being aboard subsided, and I even enjoyed the experience. My confidence growing, I attempted to turn around and see where we were going, only to feel the boat lurch beneath me as I did so. I froze rigid, unsure whether I was about to be pitched into the water and lost, before I realised that the movement had perturbed no-one else. Chambers was still gazing out over the side, lost in thought, while Lovett appeared to be asleep with his head resting on his luggage. The motion of the boat did not subside, however, and I realised we must have left the Bristol Channel and entered the ocean proper. The thought of the depth of the water beneath me made me shiver, and I sank slowly back into my seated position, all curiosity about our route or destination evaporating.

I am told the trip only lasted a half-hour, but I lost track of time completely. Every wobbling movement of the boat disoriented me, every time we crested a wave, only to descend the other side, my stomach lurched in sympathy. I tried closing my eyes but found that only amplified the effect, so instead I fixed my gaze on the man at the tiller. He projected such an air of calm, of being a man in his element, that I had to trust that all was well despite the opinions of my body.

Just when I was sure I could endure no more, The tiller-man raised an arm. "There she is," he said, and I risked turning my head to see. Immediately I felt nausea rising, and swallowed down hard. I looked at my feet, barely visible in the diffuse moonlight, and breathed deeply to combat the discomfort. I saw almost nothing of our ship until we were alongside, and ropes were being thrown down to us to secure our tiny boat.

The wall of wooden planks stretched upwards and outwards, masking the rest of the vessel from view. One by one, we ascended a rope-ladder strung from the ship with no small difficulty. The ladder amplified every movement I made, and I swung around like a sack of potatoes, bumping into the side of the ship more than once as I climbed. Fortunately, even bashing into the wood couldn't loosen my death-grip on the ropes, and I reached the top with only minor abrasions and what would develop into blisters on my hands. Arms reached out as I neared the railing at the top, and bodily lifted me over the side and deposited me more or less gently onto the deck. I gathered my breath for a moment before lifting myself onto my aching limbs and watching Amy's much more graceful ascent.

She seemed to have a knack for timing her movements with the natural swing of the ladder and scaled the climb as languidly as a cat. When she reached the top, I hurried to offer my arm for support, and she clambered over the rail to stand beside me. "How exciting!" she said, gasping for breath. I had not yet recovered the ability to speak, and hoped that she could see my smile in the dim light of the ship's lanterns.

Once we were all aboard, sailers hauled our bags up by block and tackle, and they showed us to our quarters. Once again, I followed some stranger through a maze of passages, to a tiny room that would be home for just a handful of days. I caught the faint scent of over-ripe bananas as we passed the hold.

## Chapter Thirteen

# Disaster

Our quarters were tiny, but once again, we were fortunate to have the cabin to ourselves. For all the superstitions of having women aboard a ship, the crew had gone out of their way to make Amy and me welcome. I would have preferred a window, but this was no cruise ship, and considerations of strength outweighed those of the crew's comfort. They assured me that only the captain himself had a porthole in his cabin, and even that a small one which did little beyond informing him of whether it was currently day or night, and if rain was falling. There would be little enough scenery to admire *en route*.

While we settled ourselves, the tender headed back to collect the last of our number, and had not returned before we had exhausted the diversions available in our tiny cabin. We returned to deck to await the arrivals and found the captain briefing his crew. He was a tall man, clean-shaven and well-spoken, quite unlike what I might have assumed prior to boarding. He and all of his crew were practically dressed, though smartly, and I wondered if they had dressed up for our benefit, or that this was their typical appearance. I stood and listened to the end of his speech, though I understood almost none of the nautical terms he was using and could barely gather the gist. As far as I could make out, this was a routine enough voyage for them, and he was laying out the route we were to follow and any ship-board duties he wished attending to. Then he pointed at the supplies we had brought aboard.

"Fresh fruit and veg," he said, to a resounding cheer. "Enough to last this voyage at least, if you don't make gluttons of yourselves. Bosun, secure the ration for the boatmen, and then the rest of you can have your pick. A little bird tells me there may even be a tot of rum per man in the next shipment, if you can all stay on your best behaviour in front of our guests." Here he nodded at Amy and me, and Chambers, who had by now joined us. "They're not used to our ways, so try not to startle them, alright men?" There was a laugh and a cheer in answer to this, and then the sailors set to work dividing up the food we had brought aboard.

"If I might have a moment of your time," the captain said to us, leading us away from his crew. "While you're welcome aboard the Minadora, there are some rules you must follow. They're for your safety, you understand. The engine compartment and any of the engineering spaces are off limits to you." I knew Chambers, ever the curious engineer, had been keen to see the workings of the ship, but held his tongue. "When we're under way, you're not to amble around unescorted. You're to have one of my men with you at all times when you're above decks, and I would advise against being up here at all if it's more than a little choppy."

"I hope it won't be any rougher than the journey over here," I said.

"It's a mill-pond out there, my man," he chuckled. "Perhaps I need not have warned you against roaming; if that voyage unsettled your stomach, then I doubt you'll emerge from your bed until we reach Canada!"

I was glad the darkness hid my blushes.

He continued. "These rules are all for good reason, I assure you. If one of you goes overboard, you won't stand a chance. The Atlantic is icy-cold, and even on a calm night like this, by the time we turned around and found you, I doubt you'd still be in a state worth saving. In rough seas you'd be underwater before you realised you'd fallen, and feeding the fish at the bottom a few moments later." We must have appeared terrified, as he laughed again. "I've never lost anyone yet," he boasted, "and if you do as you are told, you'll not trouble that record. You can stay now, while we bring your colleagues aboard. There's plenty of us around, we're not under steam, and I believe even such land-dwellers as yourselves can handle these rough waters!" He clapped me on the back at this last comment, and I grinned wryly. If I could avoid running into this man again before the end of the voyage, it would still be too soon.

A commotion drew our attention. Was the tender returning? Ice ran through my veins when I heard the cry from the crow's nest.

"Martian!"

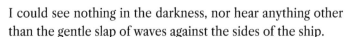

I could see nothing in the darkness, nor hear anything other than the gentle slap of waves against the sides of the ship.

The captain ran to the railing, following the lookout's raised arm. He raised a pair of binoculars from the string around his neck and swore loudly. "Sorry, ma'am," he said to Amy, then barked orders to his crew. "Connors, get this stuff stowed. McFadden, how are the boilers?"

A thin man with a Scottish accent replied. "Almost up to pressure, sir, we were preparing for the off, anyway. We're not ready to go and meet them, though."

"I don't want to approach that thing. Pile on more coal, still, we might have need of a little extra burst. The rest of you," every man on deck snapped to attention, "be ready to secure the tender when it comes alongside. I can't think this Martian is here by coincidence, so they must have spotted us. If we have to, we'll tow them along behind us until we're sure we're safe."

"Are we safe here, Captain?" I asked when the crew dashed off to their stations. "I believe you're moored out of range, are you not?"

He nodded grimly. "They've shown no interest in coming this far out, but in pursuit of a prize, who can say?"

"They can't swim, though," Amy said. There was the barest tremor in her voice.

"Not as far as we know, ma'am, no. But they tell me those things are air-tight, and that makes them watertight too. Whether they can float isn't something I wish to gamble on, but I'm more afraid of that heat-ray."

"The effective range is a thousand yards," Chambers told him. "Give or take."

"Let's hope its take. Now, I suggest you get below decks, unless you want to get involved?"

Chambers and I volunteered to assist, and they assigned us to hauling up the deliveries by rope when they arrived. I urged Amy to head down to our cabin, but she objected.

"I have some medical experience," she told the captain, "if you have a sick-bay I can be ready for any wounded we might receive?"

"If that thing catches them in the water, I doubt there'll be any wounded left. But we have some supplies. I can't spare anyone to show you where it is, though."

"Give me directions, I will find it," she said, and once he had done so, she left at a run.

---

"Any sign of the tender?" the captain called up to the crow's nest.

"I think I see her lantern," came the reply. "They're ahead of the Martian, rowing like billy-oh."

"How far?"

"You should see them soon," the lookout called. "At nine o'clock, the Martian's at ten."

We all trained our eyes on the horizon, straining to glimpse the lantern in the bows of the boat. I remembered a trick Ogilvy had shown me once, when we were trying to spot a comet in the night sky.

"Your peripheral vision is better at spotting dim things," he had said, "so keep the area you're searching just out of your main eye-line."

Just as it had then, his advice worked for me now. "There!" I called, catching the merest glimmer of lamplight. Moments later, everyone had seen it. The deck erupted into activity, rope ladders were flung over the side to dangle just above the waves, and they gathered all the lamps on deck in one place so the crew of the tender wouldn't have to strain to find us.

"Aren't we taking an awful risk showing ourselves like that?" I wondered aloud.

"If the tender doesn't see us, they're lost," Chambers said. "And if they do, the Martian can just follow them. We're not making things worse."

"Do you have any weapons, captain?" I asked.

"I wish to God we had cannons," he replied. "Only small arms, some rifles, and a shotgun. Might as well try to repel that bastard with a pea-shooter. Now, let's focus."

The tender was making what to my eyes was painfully slow progress across the ocean, though as they drew nearer I could hear the splash of the oars and the chanting of the crew as they piled on all speed that they could. Compared to the leisurely pace with which they'd brought us aboard, this was a breakneck speed.

Once again, the corner of my eye let me know of an approaching light. This time there were two, a sickly greenish-yellow, and for a heart-stopping moment I thought there were a pair of Martians come to assault us. Then shapes resolved, and I understood I was looking at what passed for eye-holes in the carapace of the fighting machine.

Surely that would impair their vision, I thought, shining lights out through their eyes. But then I remembered the demonstrations in Chambers' London basement, and that the Martians used a form of viewing screen to show them the world outside their machine. For all I knew, this glow was the byproduct of that technology, or some means by which they illuminated the darkness with light almost invisible to our eyes.

They were drawing closer.

"Will they make it?" I asked, though I'm not sure who I expected to answer. I could not tell the relative distances of the various sources of lights, nor could I judge their speeds. The Martian's 'eyes' (for that's what they resembled) were so much larger than the minuscule lantern swaying aboard the tender that they appeared to loom over it menacingly. Their height above the horizon as the Martian waded out to sea, not to mention the swaying motion the creature's movement imparted, rendered any estimate futile. Amy returned, her arms clutching bandages and gauze, and took up position beside me.

"Stand ready," the captain called, and I hoped that this meant the men were close by. Then, slightly above and beside the glowing triangular eyes, there started a pale orange glow. I squinted to bring it into focus, but as it rapidly brightened and bloomed into a fierce yellow sun, I realised with horror what it meant.

"Heat-ray!" I cried out, and everyone on the deck dived for cover. Amy and I flattened ourselves on the planks beneath us, and half-crawled, half-clambered to press our backs against the side of the ship. A glow illuminated us, allowing me to watch the crew similarly cowering for safety behind the boxes and hatch-covers that spotted the deck.

I smelt smoke and heard the crackling of fire; apart from that, the attack took place in a peculiar silence. A crate in front of me grew so bright it was hard to look at, so accustomed were my eyes to the night, but I observed as it began to blacken and blister. The planks at my back were still cool to the touch, and I could only hope that the Martian was still far enough away that the heat-ray was more terrifying than it was effective.

After a few seconds, the light faded, and it left me blinking in the darkness. Purple and green spots swam in front of my eyes, and I rubbed at them futilely. The captain must have had better sense than to look around himself, as through the afterimages I watched him raise himself and peer over the railing.

He swore again and called to his crew. "Lights! Fetch the lights!" A flurry of activity greeted his cries, and within moments there were lanterns festooned over the side of the ship. I stood and gazed out to catch a sight of our foe.

There was still a dull reddish glow beside those infernal eye-holes, as the projector of the heat-ray cooled from its intense temperatures. And now that my night vision was returning, I looked about for the wavering lantern of the ship's tender.

I saw only small flames. Fragments of the boat still burning as they bobbed on the water. The beams from the lamps illuminated coils of steam still rising from the ocean's surface, but of the boat and her crew there was no sign.

<hr />

"Full speed," the captain ordered with resignation in his voice. His second ran off to pass along the order.

"Should we not search for survivors?" I asked.

"They had whistles," he replied. "If they had breath in their lungs, they'd be blowing them fit to wake the dead. I didn't even hear a scream; they were gone in an instant."

"Even so, they might be injured, treading water..." The ship juddered beneath us, and I stumbled. "We can't leave them!"

"There's no-one to leave," the captain turned to face me. "And if we pause another moment, we'll be joining them in hell." He turned on his heel and ran to the bridge.

Amy's hand slipped into mine, and she pulled me towards the ladder down to the lower deck. "Come along," she said, "there is nothing for us to do here. And if it fires again, we don't want to be exposed." I let myself be drawn along, but instead of our quarters, she led me to the galley. "We should be able to see from here," she explained. "And we're closer to the waterline, so the risk of fire must be lower."

From the tiny porthole we took turns watching the baleful eyes of the Martian as the ship gathered speed. I could not tell for certain whether we were increasing the distance between us, or whether it was closing the gap until Amy took her turn at the window. When I next returned to look, I was sure that the eyes were smaller and closer together. We were getting away.

The glow came from the heat-ray projector again, and we moved aside from the porthole. A blinding yellow disc of light was projected on the opposite wall, but the wooden planks didn't smoulder. Against common sense, I placed the back of my hand into the beam, and snatched it back—the heat was surprising, like touching a kettle that you hadn't realised had just been used.

"Are you hurt?" Amy asked, and reached for my hand.

"Merely startled," I said, rubbing my skin. "I've had worse from a candle."

When the beam abated once more, we peered out to see the Martian vanishing below the horizon, and breathed a hearty sigh of relief.

# Chapter Fourteen

# Jury

My brother Frederick was not idle back at the base in Wiltshire while we were at sea. His own recollections of the time we spent apart were most illuminating, and I have included them in my narrative. They appear in their proper place and time, though of course I learned none of these details until our return.

The arrival of the elderly would-be collaborators caused a greater stir than I had witnessed, since I was so wrapped up in our own hasty preparations for departure. Shortly after our embarkation, Frederick announced he would place them on trial for their crimes against their fellow man.

Even this simple decision rocked the compact community. The majority, naturally, were in favour of the trial, although it was difficult to determine what the charges might be. Russell, of course, had his own opinions, and wished for the trial to be conducted under the auspices of the military.

"We are at war," he proclaimed to much assent. "These individuals assisted the enemy, betraying their fellow men and leading them to their deaths. It's a simple matter to determine their guilt, and the clear penalty is death."

Calmer heads protested that as they were non-combatants, and not enlisted in the armed forces, that a military court could have no jurisdiction over them. Russell argued they were acting as agents of the enemy and could, therefore, be classified as enemy combatants.

"In which case," Frederick pointed out, "the Hague Convention would cover them, and they would therefore be prisoners of war. That means they must be treated kindly, and cannot be summarily executed."

"Poppycock," Russell spluttered. "The Martians have violated every one of those conventions, so why should we choose to constrain ourselves to them?"

"Because we are not the Martians. We are British, and we swore to observe the rules of war. Unless you have a convincing argument that they enlisted with the enemy, then I believe they must be treated as civilians, and tried as such."

"How could they have enlisted, we have no communication with the enemy? No common language or understanding, they are in all senses of the word, utterly alien."

"Precisely," my brother replied. "So they are subject to the laws of the land, and not the military."

With Russell's grudging acceptance, they decided to hold a trial with a limited jury. While there were concerns over the ability to find anyone impartial enough to serve on the jury, or even to act as a barrister for the accused, events would soon prove that there were those who not only believed the elderly couple were innocent, but supported their actions.

<hr />

Mabel and Arthur were being held in a deep portion of the mine. Two soldiers with handguns guarded the only corridor leading in and out. There was a constant stream of curiosity seekers, 'come to view the traitors', who had to be turned away. Most of these went quietly, though a few with darker purpose in their hearts became frustrated when prevented from passing. More than a few scuffles broke out when a would-be assassin was prevented from completing his goals, and on one occasion, a guard was forced to fire a warning shot over the heads of a couple of troublemakers. Unfortunately, in a confined space, such a shot can be far from harmless, and the bullet ricocheted down the corridor. Fragments of stone splintered from the rock with each impact until the round finally came to rest. Mercifully, it injured no-one, but it became necessary to increase the number of guards.

More worrying was the explosion of graffiti. It began with a few hastily scrawled mottos, mainly variations of 'Kill Them', painted in whitewash on random walls in quiet areas. But before long, further messages in a deep red paint appeared. 'Free the faithful', was a common theme, as was 'Praise our Lords and Masters'. Frederick had not heard such overtly religious opinions since before the invasion, when I had mentioned the man at Speaker's Corner, and the cult-like group I had encountered in Woking.

The existence of such people in the last refuge was deeply concerning. The rough nature of the graffiti made it impossible to determine if all the writing was the work of the same hand, or whether there were multiple vandals at work. These slogans reappeared as quickly as they were removed and were never in the same place twice. Efforts to catch someone in the act were fruitless, and my brother was at a loss to work out how to deal with the issue.

Everyone in the mine was clearly aware of the messages, and rumours were spreading. Already there were reports of people turning on each other out of suspicion, bed-spaces rifled through for signs of red paint, and witch hunts were starting among those who failed to declare their beliefs in

Man's superiority loudly enough. Something had to be done, and quickly.

Any kind of denouncement risked stoking the fires further, but simply ignoring the issue was not a possibility. With a flash of the genius I had always seen in him, Frederick came to the solution.

"The trial will begin tonight," he announced over breakfast. Cheers broke out throughout the dining room, and he strained unsuccessfully to see if anyone failed to join in. "I shall be acting as judge, since we have no actual magistrate available to us. Three jurors will be selected at random and questioned by the solicitors on either side. If they have no objections, those people will serve. If any or all are rejected, we will draw a ballot for the replacements until we have a quorum."

"Where will it be?" a voice called out.

"Can we watch?" cried another, to general assent.

Frederick raised his arms for quiet, and it was a mark of his imposing presence that he received it. "Once the jury is selected, we will draw an additional lot of twelve observers." Complaints and groans broke out everywhere, and he appealed for calm once more. It took longer this time. "Any more, and we risk disruption. These dozen will see that justice is done: swiftly, honourably and correctly. I should add, any attempt to induce me to include your name in the observers will cause your immediate removal from the ballot. Let fortune take her course."

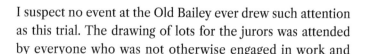

I suspect no event at the Old Bailey ever drew such attention as this trial. The drawing of lots for the jurors was attended by everyone who was not otherwise engaged in work and more than a few who ought to have been busy elsewhere. The refectory was the only area large enough to contain so many people, and it had been necessary even then to stack the tables and chairs along the sides of the cavern to allow sufficient standing room. Frederick stood behind the one remaining table, a soldier flanking him on each side as if expecting trouble. A grimy steel bucket sat on the table before him, into which he had placed the name of every eligible man and woman, each on their own slip of paper. Frederick had been reluctant to allow women to be considered for the role, as they had never been permitted to take part in trials before the invasion. His advisors reminded him that with such a small fragment of humanity at his disposal, to limit the pool of potential jurors still further was not sensible. Since my brother had already decided that he would remove the names of any he thought unsuitable for the role ahead of time, this argument convinced him to permit the inclusion of the fairer half of the population.

How odd that the Martians had inadvertently granted such rights to women when the suffragettes had failed!

Frederick never revealed to anyone that he had 'edited' the list of potential jurors until he confided in me upon my return. He explained he felt it necessary to exclude the more radical sorts on either margin, lest they pollute the minds of their fellow jurors or disrupt proceedings. When I protested at this interference in the workings of the law, he objected.

"I am confident the advocates for one or both sides would have rejected these individuals. They could never have served. But the selection and then rejection of them might have caused further dissent among those who shared their views and who would feel they had been silenced. Not to mention the additional delays inherent in selecting new jurors, vetting them too, and perhaps endless rounds of such…

The mob was baying for justice, and justice I gave them. I had promised the trial to begin that night; to delay it would have risked insurrection, almost as much as denying it."

His mind was at peace with his decision. He had prevented a greater evil by employing a lesser one, and the result had been the same for the accused. While I could not countenance such abandonment of our historical principles, I am not confident I would have had the fortitude to resist the same conclusion.

With grand ceremony, Frederick drew slips of paper from the bucket. He would unfold it, show it to the two soldiers for confirmation, and read the name aloud. As soon as each name was called, another pair of soldiers located the 'fortunate' soul and brought them through the crowd to the front of the room. Each was accompanied by a cheer from their friends, or boos and hisses from those who had not been selected, and only a few moments after beginning, the three jurors were chosen.

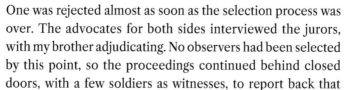

One was rejected almost as soon as the selection process was over. The advocates for both sides interviewed the jurors, with my brother adjudicating. No observers had been selected by this point, so the proceedings continued behind closed doors, with a few soldiers as witnesses, to report back that everything had been legitimate.

Miss Grace Batting was a clerk in the civil service, and a small, demure woman of the sort you could easily overlook in a crowd. She had the good fortune to be accompanying her boss on a visit to the base when hostilities had broken out, and had been found accommodation in the underground facilities. While Mr Searle, the advocate for the defence, was questioning her she seemed friendly, familiar to a degree that raised the suspicions of more than a few.

Under cross-examination, she was much less forthcoming, staring at her feet and mumbling her replies. Such a change in demeanour required an explanation, and Mr Wharton for the prosecution pressed her for one.

"Do you know Mr Searle?" he asked casually.

Miss Batting nodded, unable to meet his eye.

"I suppose you know a good many of the people here," he continued. "We are a small community, after all, and you assist our government. No doubt you have met everyone in the room before."

She shook her head, still staring at her feet.

"No?" Mr Wharton acted surprised. "I know you and I have never met, but surely you know the rest of these gentlemen?"

Again, a shake of the head.

"Look carefully, Miss Batting."

The woman lifted her head as slowly as if it were weighed down. She glanced quickly around the room, and when her eyes landed on Mr Searle, she blushed, and her eyes flashed back to the floor.

"How did you and Mr Searle meet, Miss Batting?" Wharton asked softly. No reply came. "Would you say your relationship is purely professional? Or perhaps..."

Her blush deepened, and Searle spluttered an objection.

Wharton turned to address my brother. "I reject this juror. And I ask that you replace Mr Searle as an advocate."

"Miss Batting, you are excused," Frederick announced. "No-one here is to speak of the reason, or any other matters you might have deduced from proceedings here today. Is that understood?" He looked sternly around the room, seeking acknowledgement from every man there. "Mr Searle, Mr Wharton, come with me."

As the three men convened in an ante-chamber, Miss Batting fled the room in tears. Any hope she might have harboured that her humiliation would remain secret did not last long, however. Before the next morning, scurrilous rumours dogged her wherever she went, and she retreated into herself even further. This turn of events emboldened the vocal minority who had rejected the idea of women serving on a jury, and they began protesting against the continued inclusion of Miss McGrath, the other female juror. Only Frederick's announcement that the protestors were now excluded from the pool of potential observers silenced the complaints, but they continued in quiet corners until long after the trial was over.

Who it was that had spoken despite my brother's adjuration was never discovered, and Miss Batting's story might well have ended miserably, hounded as she was by the judgement of those who had never even heard her name before that day. By the time I returned, however, Mr Searle had made an honest woman of her. While this did not stop the most vicious of the rumour-mongers, it defused the situation effectively. Their tale had become that of secret lovers, a relationship thrust into the spotlight amid the 'trial of the century', by random chance.

Frederick admitted this last part was the most fortuitous for him. Any suspicion that the draw might have been pre-selected or manipulated evaporated, since no-one would have arranged such a scandal on purpose.

## Chapter Fifteen

# Voyage

I did not sleep well that night. Visions of flaming planks flashed before me whenever I closed my eyes, and when exhaustion finally overtook me I was plagued by nightmares of men strolling about on deck, unaware that they were burning like bonfires. The rocking of the ship beneath me did not help either, though at least it was gentle and slow enough not to induce sickness.

We have all had the experience of the first night in a new location, where your hosts sleep soundly despite the noises of the house settling, or the other members of the neighbourhood going about their business. The familiar becomes so recognised, so calming, that the absence of such noises wakes them. Meanwhile the guest jumps at every rattle of the plumbing or creak of a step. So it was with the sounds of the ship, although to a much greater degree. Instead of a squeaky step you had the spine of the ship groaning as the waves passed beneath it. The bang of air trapped in the plumbing was nothing compared to the splashing of water just inches from my head on the other side of a few thin planks. And the barely muffled voices of the crew woke me more than once, convinced an intruder had entered our bedroom.

The darkness of the cabin was oppressive in its own way. I realised I had never experienced such a true absence of light before. Even on the darkest of nights there is enough glow from a gas lamp outside or the moon and stars to see at least vague shadows of shapes. But this was so intense I could not tell whether or not my eyes were open. I would have lit a lamp or a candle if I had trusted my ability to find and light them in the pitch black without starting a fire, but another part of me also mocked my need for a night light, as if I were some small child afraid of monsters under the bed.

Eventually I heard sounds from outside the cabin that suggested more activity than had been occurring overnight. I dressed as best as I could manage in the dark and eased the door open as quietly as I could to avoid disturbing Amy. The corridor was lit with a lamp, dazzlingly bright after the stygian interior of our room. I closed the door behind me, and went in search of information.

I found most of the crew at breakfast in the galley, though the captain was not among them. Each man was ploughing his way through a plate of bacon and a singular grilled tomato each, the latter having been part of the fresh goods we brought aboard the day before. The dim light of dawn was insinuating its way through the small porthole over the long table.

I sat down, and the ship's cook placed a similar plate in front of me. The scent of the fried bacon awoke my hunger, and I set to work demolishing the food with gusto. Not a word was spoken around the table while we consumed the meal, but this silence continued on after the last morsel was devoured and the clatter of knives and forks had ceased. I remembered these men had also lost three of their colleagues last night.

I had not known the men from Wiltshire before we had set off, and I had not learned their names on the brief journey to

Bristol. My grief was therefore not as sharp as it might have been, though I confess I might still have been numbed by the loss of so many of the original camp in Shropshire. I was glad that Amy and Chambers had both been along with me, and that we had made it aboard without loss.

The captain entered along with Chambers, and I immediately bombarded him with questions about our escape the previous night.

"God's teeth, man, let me eat first. We're alive, is that not enough for now?"

I had to bite my tongue to keep from reminding him that not all of our number had in fact survived. Perhaps as a man of action, unlike myself, this was his method of dealing with loss. Any grief that he felt had not affected his appetite, and he finished his breakfast in short order.

He leaned back with a belch, and fixed me with a glare. I shifted in my chair, unsure whether I should be waiting for him to speak, or if this was my invitation to begin my questioning. I concluded he was not about to break the awkward silence, and I cleared my throat.

"Captain, I am sorry for the loss of your men," I began, and the room chilled around me. I ploughed on regardless. "In addition, the supplies we were bringing for you." The temperature dropped still further.

"Most of the provisions we brought for your good selves were in the first boat-load," Chambers interjected. "The losses fall mainly on us, as they do with the personnel. Apart from the rum we were planning to reward you with."

"So you'll be wanting to raid our hold, is that it?" a voice came from the back of the room.

"Not at all," Chambers said. I had been about to ask for exactly that, but he had not let me speak. "The terms of our arrangement have not altered, we thank you for giving us passage, and I can only assure you that the mission upon which we are embarked is vital to the war effort."

"And what would that be?" the captain asked. "What was worth the lives of three of my men?"

"And five of ours," Chambers said. "We are striving for a weapon that will turn the tide in our favour. I wish I could tell you more, but I am sure you understand we are sworn to utter secrecy."

A chorus of dissent greeted this. I bolstered Chambers' attempts at diplomacy.

"We know you are men of honour," I said, ignoring the scoffs that came from the men. "But if the Martians should capture one of you, the less you know the better for all of us. Our lost men knew only that they were assisting the fight, nothing more, and they gave their all without ever understanding their part in it. All we ask is that you trust us."

"And lay down our own lives, if you say so?"

Chambers shook his head. "I do not intend to ask for that," he said. "You have no tender, no boat to take us ashore. So the men we are meeting will have to shoulder the risks of transporting us. They will come out to meet the Minadora, and take us ashore. They will then return us, with our prize, when we are successful."

"And will they also bring us the missing goods you promised us?" I did not see who made this comment, but it was met with a hearty cheer.

"You're missing very little of that," Chambers began, but the crew soon drowned him out.

"We shall do what we can," I shouted above the mob. "Once we are in radio range, we will explain the situation and appeal to their good nature. I am sure they will make up the shortfall."

Chambers gave me a stare at this, but I had no regrets. If the Canadians would make me a liar when we arrived, I would deal with the situation then. For now, we needed these men on our side.

"Now, Captain," I said. "Perhaps you can regale us with the tale of how you expertly escaped the Martians last night?"

He eyed me sceptically, but I held my face in a gentle smile that displayed no guile, and he took my flattery at face value.

He took up the next thirty minutes with a blow-by-blow account of our flight from the Martian, with interjections from all sides and much good-natured disagreement between the men over the precise order of things. Suffice it to say that we outpaced the Martian by the captain's good sense in having the boilers up to pressure early, allowing us to pile on speed as soon as the situation allowed.

The most junior man aboard had a most disconcerting revelation to share with us. I believe they originally employed him as a cabin-boy, but now had additional duties because of the ship being understaffed. They had positioned him on the starboard side of the ship, ready to haul in the anchor, when the Martian appeared. As such, he had no other duties to distract him until the call to raise the anchor came, and watched the approaching fighting machine with his young eyes.

"It grew, I tell you," he said. "As it came closer, it lifted itself still further out of the water, like it was on stilts!" The other men laughed at him, but his words had the ring of truth about them.

I probed him for more details. "Had you ever seen one before?" He shook his head, they had been at sea when the attack came, so how could he have done? "So you've never seen their legs?"

"I had a glimpse as it rose," he said, "long, spindly things they were, like a spider. I'm amazed they could take the weight."

Chambers took over the interrogation, being more familiar with the anatomy of the machines. "How big around do you suppose it was, each leg?"

"I couldn't say, sir, it was dark and a long ways off. But I saw the knees, they looked knobbly to me, too big for its bones, if you see what I mean."

Whenever I had seen a tripod marching about it had always looked in proportion. The knee-joint was slightly wider than the leg above and below, but not by much. Was this some new variant?

The boy continued. "There were two stalks coming down from the top of it, then they fused into one. The same thing happened beneath the knee, or at least I think so. I couldn't see the join because of the water."

I couldn't picture this at all, but Chambers grabbed a pencil and scrap of paper from the navigator and sketched something. "Like this?" he said, pushing it over to the lad.

"That's it!" he cried.

I looked at the paper. Chambers had sketched a mere oval as the body of the thing, and a single leg - I recognised it as the same mechanism by which a tripod for a surveyor or a photographer extended, a single element sliding between two others. Two parallel beams projected downwards, like the twin bones of a man's forearm, before the gap between them was filled by the top of a single beam which continued downwards, leaving the other two behind.

"It grew," Chambers murmured.

Chambers and I each retired to his own quarters to contemplate this development. Were all the fighting machines able to do this? Why had we not seen it before? Perhaps they had never needed to extend their legs, although it would have made sense when covering uneven or difficult terrain. Then again, raising the centre of gravity of the thing might make it too unstable, they might reserve such a manoeuvre for dire situations.

"At least it suggests they cannot swim," I told Amy when she awoke. "That thing was still walking, albeit in deeper water than we might have expected. But it means there is a limit to their range at sea."

"So we stick to deeper waters," she said. "Bad for your nerves, but then so would be one of those things bearing down on us."

"My nerves are fine, thank you," I said. "At least now we're inside. I can trick myself into believing I'm back in that cart on a bumpy road while in here, and not consider the abyss beneath."

"So you won't be joining me on deck?" she smiled. "I feel the need for fresh air, after a night without a window to open."

"I will join you for breakfast," I replied, "and see how it goes from there."

I drank tea while Amy breakfasted on toast and jam, eschewing the bacon offered by the cook so politely I think he was grateful to have been allowed to suggest it.

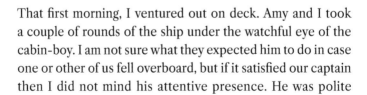

That first morning, I ventured out on deck. Amy and I took a couple of rounds of the ship under the watchful eye of the cabin-boy. I am not sure what they expected him to do in case one or other of us fell overboard, but if it satisfied our captain then I did not mind his attentive presence. He was polite enough to keep a suitable distance to allow us to converse in private, without being so far away that someone might accuse him of shirking his duties.

Not that Amy and I had much to discuss that morning. The narrowness of our escape, and the losses that had ensued, was not something either of us wished to dwell on. The journey ahead held so many unknowns that any speculation would be futile, and so we found ourselves engaged in the most peculiar type of small-talk that would have bored us both senseless before the invasion.

After our second trip around the deck I remarked upon the weather. Such a British thing to do, I know, but there were clouds building on the horizon in the direction we were head-ing, and almost without thinking I said "it looks as if a storm is brewing." We stood and gazed at the looming formation, and I realised that the relative smoothness of our voyage that I had enjoyed so far was ending.

---

I didn't leave our cabin for two days.

Amy brought me small, light meals, which I could not bring myself to touch. She urged me to eat, but every slight move-ment of the ship, or even my head, was enough to bring on another wave of the nausea. It was all I could do to swallow the occasional mouthful of water to remove the foul taste my sickness left behind. I have never felt so ill in my life, and was for a while certain that something I had eaten must have been responsible. Only the continued good health of the rest of the crew and passengers convinced me that my malady was due to my inability to function on a moving vessel.

Finally the ceaseless pitching and rolling diminished to a point that I could lie down long enough to fall asleep, and when I awoke some untold hours later, my appetite had returned. Accustomed to a lingering malaise after such a debilitating bout of illness, I was astonished that I felt myself again, and so quickly. A round of cheers from my fellow passengers, and a few nods from the crew greeted my smiling face at the galley door. They had the decency to let me finish two full plates before their good-natured ribbing began.

"You were so green I wasn't sure whether to send you to your bunk or to plant you!" the first mate said, to open the mockery. I then grinned and endured a good ten minutes of what I presumed to be well-worn jokes at the expense of the land-lubber I had proven myself to be. Eventually they ran out of material, and departed to their various duties.

The captain poked his head in, and I braced myself for another round of hilarity.

"Feeling better, I see?" he said kindly, before sitting down beside me and helping himself to the last slice of bread I had given up on finishing. "Next time, eat something, it helps. Believe me." He stood to leave, but I had to know.

"You sound as if you speak from experience, sir," I said.

"My first voyage, on a clipper," he mused. "We ran into in the tail end of a hurricane that had lashed the Bahamas, and couldn't raise the sails until it was done with us. I was barely seventeen, and spent about three days feeding the fish over the side. The midshipman thought he might cheer me up by telling me that no-one ever died of sea-sickness." He shook his head. "It was only the hope of dying that was keeping me alive," he said, with a chuckle. "You get used to it, grow your sea-legs." He left the room, and I hoped against hope that I wouldn't have another opportunity to find out for myself.

## Chapter Sixteen

# Trial

A third juror was swiftly selected, and no objections were raised to their inclusion. We now had our impartial decision-makers, and they were sequestered away from the rest of the camp to avoid being exposed to any influence or intimidation by those who had already made up their minds. Nevertheless, they had already become as famous as any star of stage or screen might have been before the war. Had the gossip magazines survived the fall, they would have had enough material to last them for weeks, examining the lives of these three individuals.

Miss McGrath had weathered the storm of anti-female sentiment and remained on the panel. A woman in her late-forties, with a prominent grey streak in her widow's peak, she had the air of a school-mistress about her. Rumours suggested that she had been married before the arrival of the Martians, but had taken the opportunity to escape an unhappy situation and present herself as a spinster instead. Her supposed husband was variously and confidently described as a violent abuser who had beaten her until she felt the need to flee, or perhaps a kingpin of the criminal network in London, or a man so unutterably dull that to spend an evening with him would be to invite death by ennui. Frederick saw no reason to question her version of events; with the destruction of almost all records, it would have been impossible to prove either way, and would have no bearing on her abilities as a juror. My brother suspected that most of the rumours were put about by those still unhappy with the inclusion of a woman, and he hoped that by ignoring them, they might fizzle out.

Mr Barker, a robust man in his thirties, had less mystery encircling him. A plain-speaking man, formerly a worker on the railways, anyone who had spent more than a few minutes in his company would be aware of his feelings and opinions on almost any matter. During questioning for the jury position, however, he had convinced both sides that he relished learning as much as possible about the case before making up his mind. The advocates attempted to draw him out, hoping to reveal some preconceived idea of whether the alleged collaborators were guilty, but he refused to accept that he could decide without hearing the facts.

"Anyone as knows me, they'll tell you," he proclaimed. "I'm swift to make up my mind, but I listen first. 'Listen and learn', my sweet mother told me, God rest her, and that's what I do."

The final juror, replacing Miss Batting, was Mr Gill. Where Miss McGrath might have suggested a school-mistress, he had been a headmaster at one of the finer public schools. His inclusion in the government's refuge had been a careful choice, the powers that be having realised that education of future generations would be essential. He was perhaps the least controversial of the selection, a man of learning and discipline, and almost all agreed that he would be a fine juror.

The jury themselves evidently agreed, nominating and electing him as their foreman.

With a jury in place, attention turned to the selection of the observers. Twelve seats had been allocated, and once more the battered bucket was brought forward. Before the drawing began, my brother addressed the crowd.

"If you are selected today, remember that this is a privilege being granted to you, and not a God-given right. You will be expected to remain silent throughout the trial, not to interrupt, interject, or otherwise disrupt proceedings. If you do, I shall have you removed from the chamber, and you may face punishment. If any of you do not agree to this requirement, let us know now and we can remove you from consideration."

Silence greeted his words.

"Very well then. Let us begin."

He stirred up the contents of the bucket, making a grand show of ensuring the selection was random, and drew the first slip of paper.

"Maxwell Thomson!" he called out. A large man with a vast, bushy moustache leapt to his feet and cried, "Here!" A polite round of applause accompanied him as he made his way to the front of the room.

Another slip of paper. "Molly Anderson!"

A squeal came from a slender woman in her twenties, who sat in the front row. She flapped her arms as she joined Mr Thomson beside the table.

And so it went on until twelve names had been picked. A diverse group of the cavern's inhabitants stood at the top of the room, shaking each other's hands and congratulating one another as if they had earned this opportunity through anything other than pure chance.. The remainder of the crowd grumbled in disappointment but did not protest. The presence of a half-dozen soldiers around the room, conspicuously but casually holding their rifles, may have had something to do with that.

"We have our observers," Frederick cried out. "No doubt they will be able to regale the rest of you with details after the trial, but we also have a secretary to take notes in shorthand, and will make a transcript available as soon as possible."

With that, they adjourned to the chamber which had been put aside for the trial - deep within the caverns, with only a single entrance and exit to guard. The accused stood in a makeshift dock, formed of three tables upturned on their sides, and arranged around them. The advocates stood behind a table each, with their notes and other paraphernalia to hand. The jury sat in three arm chairs along one side wall, opposite the dock, and the observers sat on hard wooden stools at the rear of the chamber.

Armed guards flanked the entrance, but a crowd gathered nonetheless. The man at the front of the crowd listened to proceedings and whispered a report back to the man behind, who repeated it down the line. By this means, a few hundred people were able to monitor the progress of the trial as it happened, although some inaccuracies built up in the repeated telling and re-telling.

Frederick called for order, and the trial began.

───◄O►───

The case for the prosecution was easily made. Statements from Amy, Chambers and myself were read into the record, and apart from a few subtle differences in the most minor of details, were identical. Of particular importance, and highlighted by Mr Wharton, were our reports of the explanations given by the collaborators as to the reasons for their behaviour.

"They make no apology," Wharton expounded. "But accepted their actions would have, as their consequence, the deaths of many. How many of our fellows, refugees from the camp in Shropshire, might have made it here if not for their intervention? It is only by the reports of these fortunate few who managed to escape that we know of this travesty, this betrayal, this treason against mankind!"

"I object," Mr Searle interrupted. "We have written statements for the prosecution, but my clients have been prevented from confronting their accusers. How convenient that they be absent, and unable to answer under cross-examination?"

"I have explained," Mr Wharton replied, "that they have been called away on matters most urgent. Vital to the very survival of our nation, if not our species."

"So you say," Searle replied. "But I put it to you that you don't wish us to examine their stories too closely."

This opinion was met with jeers from the observers, and as word was relayed to the crowd beyond, a chorus of boos and hisses echoed down the corridors.

My brother called for calm. When it finally arrived, he stood and addressed the court. "These witnesses are risking life and limb for their country, and so we must make do with their sworn testimony. I remind all parties that this is a perfectly legal arrangement. The jury must weigh the evidence provided by both sides and not draw conclusions from the appearance or otherwise of a witness." He sat back down and indicated that the trial could continue.

Mr Searle shuffled the papers on the table in front of him. "Not all the witnesses are absent."

Another disturbance passed through the chamber, but Frederick's upraised arm brought silence back once more.

"Mrs Chambers is here, I believe? In the caverns, I mean, not the courtroom."

"Your honour," Mr Wharton said, "Mrs Chambers has requested not to be involved in the trial. She was so strongly affected by the events in question that she cannot bring herself to face revisiting them."

"Another convenience," Mr Searle snapped. "A little alleged unpleasantness over a cup of tea hardly compares to the risk of death to my clients. They deserve a fair trial!"

Frederick slammed his hands on the table and stood once more. Silence fell immediately over the room. "If you are suggesting that I am presiding over some kind of show trial, I will find you in contempt."

Mr Searle muttered a retraction and shook his head.

"Now, should you have a legal objection, I will hear it," Frederick continued. "We have three sworn testimonies under oath. Do you have any valid reason to keep them from the court?"

Searle again shook his head.

"You will get your chance to argue your own case in a moment. Mr Wharton will answer any questions you have about the testimonies, and your clients have the right to address the court. I will grant them this opportunity in due course. If there are no further objections, then, Mr Wharton, you may proceed."

"Thank you, your honour." Wharton bowed slightly, caught himself, and stood bolt upright again. "We have three testimonies: all agree that the accused confessed to the crimes of which they are now charged; all agree that the accused, while elderly, are not so infirm that they failed to understand the consequences of their actions; and all agree that they barely escaped with their lives. I submit that the standard of proof has been exceeded, and that these two—" he gestured towards Mabel and Arthur in the dock "—are guilty."

A round of applause broke out among the observers, and cheers were heard from the corridors outside. Wharton sat, looking satisfied with his performance, but solemn as the situation dictated.

"Mr Searle," Frederick called. "Your statement, please."

Chapter Seventeen

# Arrival

The last few days of our voyage were calmer, and my illness did not return. Whether I was indeed more accustomed to the movements of the ship or that it had just settled down sufficiently to not distress me, I knew and cared not. I was well enough to overcome my fear of the abyss and circumnavigate the deck with Amy twice a day, enjoy the freshness of the sea air and feel the cool breeze on my face. For that brief period, I could almost understand how men fell in love with the ocean, and would happily put to sea for weeks or months at a time. Then I remembered that more days than not were storm-tossed and violent, and I counted the hours until our arrival on solid land once more.

One interesting diversion was the navigation performed by the first officer. During the day, he would use a sextant to measure the angle of the sun above the horizon, after which a consultation in various tables and charts would give our latitude above the equator. This varied little, day by day, as our destination was at a similar northern degree. Our longitude was calculated by determining the moment at which the sun reached its zenith, the so-called 'local noon', and then referring to a clock set to the time at Greenwich to determine how far behind we were. Each hour meant fifteen degrees of longitude, with each minute being a fraction of that. Confusingly, the divisions of a degree were also called minutes and seconds, but you could not simply transpose one for the other. After a little practice, however, I became quite adept at the conversion, and on our last day at sea, the first officer allowed me to perform the entire procedure, from measurement to plotting our location on the charts in his office. I derived a huge measure of satisfaction when he repeated the process and confirmed that I had calculated correctly.

I had longed for the first sight of land, but naturally prudence dictated that we lower our anchor while Newfoundland was still beyond the horizon. Too far, and we should never be reached by boat; while if we strayed too close, we might attract unwelcome attention from the Martians we knew had also colonised this land. Thus, our navigation was required to be extremely precise, and I was glad to forego such important work, leaving it up to the expert.

For the last day or so of the trip, the radio operator had been calling the base regularly, but had failed to elicit a response. My anxiety had risen with each failed attempt, but he assured me that this did not necessarily mean anything disastrous had happened. Quite apart from the base wanting to limit transmissions to avoid discovery, there were other reasons why we might not be able to make contact.

"The atmosphere plays a part," he reminded me. "The weather makes the radio waves bounce all over. Some days we can hear them from as far as Greenland, some days you'd do better waving flags at 'em."

I recalled our own radio troubles at the camp in Shropshire, and couldn't help but worry that the Martians might once again be jamming our signals. There was no repeat of the strange whistling up and down the band that we had heard then, however, so I held out hope.

Now that we could no longer draw closer to shore, we had to hope that conditions allowed for communication once more. We had no boat to set out on our own, and even if we had, the captain would never have authorised a launch unless we had the all-clear from land.

Shortly before sunset, the radio-man's calls were answered. Faintly at first, but then gradually louder and more clearly, the voice on the other end came through. Practically the entire crew bundled into the tiny radio room to hear, before the captain ordered them all back to their stations. Chambers and I were permitted to stay as delegates of the mission.

"Minadora, we hear you," the voice called. "Say your condition, over."

"Moored at rendezvous," the operator replied. "Lost our tender, so we need you to come and fetch your guests."

"Stand by," came the reply. There then followed a lengthy period of waiting, punctuated only by static from the radio. My leg jittered beneath me as the minutes ticked by. Eventually, the voice returned. "Expect us at 19:30," he said. "Three flashes of the lantern. Out."

"Be sure to ask them about those supplies," the captain said to me as I descended the ladder into the boat. "I shall be holding you to your promise."

I assured him that I would, although privately my immediate concern was on making it to dry land in one piece. The Canadians had assured us that they would not permit the tender to set off if there was any danger of a Martian attack, but that did not prevent us all from watching the horizon intently as we boarded the boat.

We only required one trip, another reminder if one were needed, that we had lost many of our number. The voyage passed without incident, and I did not even feel unwell at the motion of the boat. Perhaps I truly was adapting to a life on the seas.

The boat fetched up on a shallow, stony beach, where a couple of burly men hauled it most of the way out of the water. We clambered out, and I almost immediately pitched over onto the stones. My legs wobbled under me in a peculiar fashion, and I realised that I was still attempting to counteract the regular motion of the ship. Only by fixing my eyes on the static horizon was I able to move around without stumbling, but whenever I glanced down to check my footing among the rocks, I felt my balance desert me. Fortunately, this strange sensation quickly passed, and I was able to keep up with the rest of the party as we made our way off the beach.

A truck awaited us, similar to the ones we had used in Shropshire. Leaning against the side of it, smoking a pipe, stood a tall, wiry man in a long, dark coat. At our arrival, he knocked out his pipe, stuffed it into a pocket, and extended a hand to shake.

Chambers, now the most senior man in the party, introduced us all.

"Tyler Armand," our contact said, with a mild French accent. "Think of me as your liaison for the duration of your visit. I'll make the necessary introductions and look after any problems or questions you might have. Shall we get going?" He gestured to the truck.

I noticed it had its headlights taped over, leaving only a narrow slit for the light to escape. "The darkness means we stand out," Armand explained. "So we try to reduce the amount of light we spill, avoid getting spotted."

I was not confident in his ability to drive with so little illumination, but given that the camp was about ten miles away, I was not going choose to walk. We climbed in and set off on the rattling journey towards yet another of mankind's last strongholds.

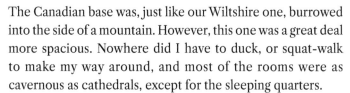

The Canadian base was, just like our Wiltshire one, burrowed into the side of a mountain. However, this one was a great deal more spacious. Nowhere did I have to duck, or squat-walk to make my way around, and most of the rooms were as cavernous as cathedrals, except for the sleeping quarters.

"We've had to dig out a lot more of those since the invasion," Armand explained, "and for obvious reasons we didn't take the effort of hollowing out giant dormitories. They might have been easier if we used explosives, but now the place is occupied, that's not an option. Besides, it'd only draw attention. So we've chipped out bunks as and when we've needed them. As guests, you won't be sharing; many of our staff are forced to hot-bunk while we expand."

"Hot-bunk?" Amy asked.

"When one man gets out of bed, another gets in," he said simply. "Three shifts a day means three men can use a single bunk. Efficient, though unpopular."

"Is that even sanitary?" I asked.

He shrugged. "Luckily, we're not short of water, so hygiene isn't a major problem. And for now at least, folks would rather put up with that than attempt to survive outside. Still, it gives them incentive to dig faster."

Chambers was keen to get started. "What of our mission?" he asked. "The sooner we start, the sooner we can be out of your hair, and free up some of what sounds like valuable bed-space."

"All in good time. Make yourselves at home, there are rations in the galley. Get some sleep if you can, and we'll bring you up to speed in the morning."

True to his word, there was food laid out in the communal area, and plenty of it. This boded well for my promise to resupply the Minadora, but for now, we tucked in and satisfied our appetites.

We adjourned for an early night, although unfortunately I could still feel the ship pitching and rolling beneath me whenever I lay down. In the pitch blackness of the cave it made no difference whether my eyes were open or closed, and eventually I pulled back the curtain separating our beds from the rest of the room a crack, to allow a sliver of light to pass inside. With that illuminating a patch of the rough wall, I could focus my eyes on something static, and finally overcome the sensation of movement. I don't know when I fell asleep, precisely, but I awoke to the sounds of my colleagues starting their day around me, feeling remarkably well rested and alert.

We made our way to breakfast in good spirits, keen to get under way with our objective. Armand joined us at the meal, and we made small-talk while enjoying the hospitality of our Canadian cousins. I was itching to get down to business, but was mindful of my new responsibility for diplomacy. If discussions of the weather, our voyage, and which foodstuffs we missed from before the war were essential to building bridges, I would play along.

By the time we had finished our food, we felt as if we had known each other for some time, so talented was Armand at putting us at our ease.

"Right then," he said, when the last of the plates was cleared away. "Shall we get to work?"

We sat together in one of the cavernous spaces, on over-stuffed armchairs that looked to have been salvaged from a gentleman's club. They were arranged in a circle on a large Axminster rug, which despite its size barely covered a fraction of the floor space of the cave. Lamps were placed around so that we found ourselves in an island of light surrounded by vast blackness. The circle of light that came through the entrance looked small and distant, and I felt we were quite isolated, able to have a private discussion without risk of being overheard.

A long, low wooden table occupied the space between us, and this was strewn with maps and papers. Clearly a great deal of preparation had been done before our arrival, so we sat back and sipped a rather fine coffee while Armand ran through the details.

He stood and paced slowly along the length of the table. "You have need of pitchblende, I understand. Or, more accurately, the element uranium that it contains."

"Correct," Chambers said. "Purifying it is another challenge, but it forms the basis of the Martians' energy sources. You know about the effects of the explosion we caused?"

Armand nodded. "The pulse that destroyed electrical equipment, not to mention the Martian machinery. Do let Mr Russell know how impressed I am that he thought of it."

I exchanged an uncomfortable look with Chambers. "I do not believe he knew what the effect would be," I said hesitantly. "The explosion would have taken out the local threat, but he was as surprised as we were that it had a wider effect."

"I was under the impression that he was your expert in such matters," Armand said.

"Oh, he is," Chambers agreed. "But such matters are relative, and this is a new science. As I said, purifying the ore will be our next challenge."

"There I have some good news," Armand said. He shuffled the papers on the table and spread out a map of the area. "We may have access to a source of the pure uranium."

"It exists in a pure form?" Chambers gasped. "We've never heard of that before, it's always been found as a salt, in small proportions in the rock."

"Not naturally, no," Armand agreed. "There are no nuggets of uranium to be found, at least as far as we know."

"So how did you find it in..." Chambers' eyes widened. "You don't mean...?"

Armand nodded. "The Martians."

"You're going to steal their power sources?" I asked.

"Oh good heavens, no," Armand laughed. "We barely have the weapons to defend ourselves if we should need to, we could never launch an assault on their bases. But the Martians are mining it, refining it, and supplying it to their factories."

Chambers grinned. "And we're going to intercept it."

## Chapter Eighteen

# Planning

"Intercept the Martians' delivery of uranium?" I asked. "You just said you don't have enough weapons for that."

"I said we don't have enough to assault them directly," Armand said. "Fortunately, we don't have to." He began marking the spots on the map as he described them. "The mine is here, at Elliot Lake. It's overseen by two fighting machines, and they patrol along this ridge-line here. It gives them a commanding view of the only clear approach by road, which comes through this choke-point."

"I can see why you wouldn't want to attack the mine," Chambers said. "They'd see you coming a mile away, and even if you somehow got in, you'd never get back out."

"Exactly," Armand agreed. "Every few days they ship out a batch, regular as clockwork. They always follow the same route, too."

"I fail to see how that helps us," I said. "It's still going to require a direct assault. We cannot take on one of their machines on the open road any more easily than in the mine."

Armand grinned. "Then it's just as well that they don't use their fighting machines to transport the cargo, isn't it?"

"Are their manipulators more vulnerable?" Chambers asked.

"Probably, but they don't use them either."

I sighed deeply. "Please stop with the riddles, and just tell us the plan."

Armand gazed at me over his half-moon glasses, but refrained from arguing. "The Martians don't transport the stuff at all. Men do."

Silence greeted this pronouncement. Despite our own run-in with those who thought they knew the Martians' motives, I could scarcely believe that there would be men who pandered to their desires so easily.

"Traitors?" Chambers asked. "Or prisoners?"

"Prisoners first and foremost," Armand replied. "Though they aid the enemy to spare their own lives, so I would still brand them as turncoats."

"You don't know what you would do to save your own life until the moment arrives," I said, trying to suppress a shudder. Amy grasped my arm with her hand, and the pain which accompanied my recollection passed.

"Perhaps not," Armand said, "but in any case, they buy themselves precious little life with their treachery. The mining is hard and dangerous work, but the refining is where the true peril lies."

An image of a man in crisp white hospital sheets, grey and sallow, flashed before my eyes. "The radiation," I said quietly.

"The workers have no protection, no shielding. It's not out of laziness that the Martians have men do the labour."

"But they must have protective equipment," I protested. "When the material gets to their factory, when they turn it into power sources, they wouldn't expose themselves to those dangers."

"Their metal alloy protects them," Chambers said. "Inside their manipulator machines, they would be safe. They could perform the entire operation without our involvement."

"And must have, on Mars," Amy pointed out. "When they produced the first of their machines."

"Perhaps they have limited supplies of that metal," Armand said. "Or perhaps the equivalent of condemned men labour there too, and suffer. Or maybe they just enjoy watching us sicken and die. In any case, they have provided us with a weakness that we shall exploit."

Regardless of the reason for using men in the production process, he was right that we had an opportunity. Observers had been watching for long enough to determine the best time to attack. The refined uranium was loaded on to a truck, and once enough had been gathered, a two-man team would drive it across country to the Martians' main base of operations.

"How much do they carry?" Chambers asked. "We'll only get one shot at this, so it had better be worth it."

"They daren't load too much," Armand said. "Too much together runs the risk of a reaction, so they place small amounts into metal cases and space them around the bed of the truck. And it's heavy too, denser than lead. If they stacked it up, it'd probably crush the wheels. Even so, there should be enough for two of your bombs each, from what you've told us."

"Each?" Chambers said. "What do you mean?"

"We're going to build our own, start our fight back," Armand said calmly. "Did you think we'd just hand it all over? You might still believe yourselves masters of the Empire, but I can tell you that those days are over now."

"Unacceptable," Chambers spluttered. "We have over two dozen machines prowling around England and the other home nations, and they're building more as we speak. Even four bombs would barely make a dent in that! And now you propose restricting us to only two? Nonsense!"

"And we have the whole of Canada to liberate, sir. It's two, or none," Armand replied, and began rolling up the map. "We have devised this plan, laid all the groundwork, and you'd never manage it without us. Whereas we can quite happily carry it out without you and keep all the spoils for ourselves."

"You forget, sir," I said, "that we alone have the designs for the bombs. Without our expertise, you would have nothing but a pile of dangerous goods."

"We are aware that you merely overloaded a power source to gain your dramatic effect. I am confident that some research will lead us to the same end result. And with twice the raw materials, we would be comfortable sparing some for investigation and experimentation. I shall let you deliberate, gentlemen. Come and find me when your decision is made." He tucked his map and papers under his arm and stalked out of the room.

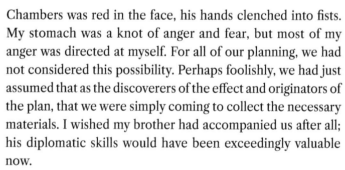

Chambers was red in the face, his hands clenched into fists. My stomach was a knot of anger and fear, but most of my anger was directed at myself. For all of our planning, we had not considered this possibility. Perhaps foolishly, we had just assumed that as the discoverers of the effect and originators of the plan, that we were simply coming to collect the necessary materials. I wished my brother had accompanied us after all; his diplomatic skills would have been exceedingly valuable now.

"We cannot submit to this, this extortion!" Chambers said once he judged Armand to be out of earshot. "They promised us the uranium we needed, and by God they should honour their word!"

"They are," Amy said, drawing a hard stare from Chambers. She continued, her voice calm and level. "Did they promise us four bombs? Two? Or even one?"

Chambers shifted awkwardly.

"Or did they offer merely to assist us with gathering ore?" Amy pressed. "As it is, we shall have enough of it for two bombs, and in an already refined state at that. You might have dreamed of more, but how much of the raw material would have fit in the hold of the Minadora? Or how much could we transport in the tenders before our luck ran out, and we were discovered? Allowing our cousins to defend themselves seems a small enough price to pay, as I see it."

"It's rewarding them for their greed," Chambers growled. "I've come here, left my family for this? I will have no part of it."

As much as I agreed with my wife, I could see Chambers' point of view. Fortunately, I had an answer. "It is not our decision to make," I pointed out. "The terms of our agreement, while they did not outline exact quantities," I nodded at Amy, "also made no mention of sharing our knowledge and information. So we must radio home and ask for instructions."

Chambers let out a huge sigh and his hands unclenched. "I intend to argue against it," he said.

"To what end?" I asked. "If Wiltshire order Armand to hand it all over, do you think he will listen? And if he does not, will they order us to remove him and assume command over this base? Or the whole of Canada, perhaps? There are barely a handful of us. If they load up the Minadora with every able-bodied man they can find, are we to go to war over this? Assuming they can find a rifle for even half of them, that is. We must fight the Martians, not each other."

"I don't like it," Chambers muttered.

"Nor do I," I agreed. "But if this works, we can do it again, and again. Imagine regular shipments of uranium arriving in Bristol, a ready supply of bombs. If we refuse now out of principle, we cut off our only supply."

Chambers' shoulders slumped, and he flopped down into his armchair. "Fine. We can radio Wiltshire tonight," he murmured.

## Chapter Nineteen

# Outburst

Searle stood for a few minutes, regarding each member of the jury in turn. Whether he meant to measure them up, judge their feelings, or impress them with an air of authority was not clear. What was clear by the awkward shifting in their seats was that the jury was uncomfortable being observed so closely.

"Mr Searle," Frederick called. "If you have any remarks to make, I would urge you to do so now."

"Yes, your honour," he said. "I believe the court will agree that we find ourselves living through remarkable times. Unprecedented, I would argue. Of course, we have not forgotten the first invasion, but that was over in a matter of days, and by any measure with a much lesser impact. What was the final death toll? Thousands? Perhaps a few tens of thousands? Even if it were ten times that, it is dwarfed by the situation today where perhaps an even smaller number are left to inhabit the earth." He paused, as if to let the scale of the catastrophe sink in.

"So killing even a single man is worse now, don't you think?" a voice called from the back of the room. Frederick appealed for silence, and the offender was rapidly ushered out.

"We are in uncharted territory," Searle continued, ignoring the outburst. "When the invasion began, panic ensued. Men fought in the streets over supplies, or for places on trains.

They trampled one another in their haste to escape. The military fired upon looters, or anyone who might have prevented their evacuation. I think every one of us here today owes his or her place in safety to the actions of others, deciding who would live and who would die. We stand here now atop a pile of bodies."

The uproar in the court and the corridors beyond was immediate and vocal. Members of the public surged forward, keen to silence such words by any means necessary. Searle recoiled from the angry mob, cowering behind one of the guards, while Frederick called for order.

"This proves my point," Searle bellowed over the jeers of the audience. "Violence is always the reaction of men in a difficult situation. When life is threatened, we allow for a plea of self-defence to justify our actions..."

"Shut up, man!" Frederick called. "Court adjourned!"

"Let he who is without sin cast the first stone!" Searle barked as he was led away by armed soldiers.

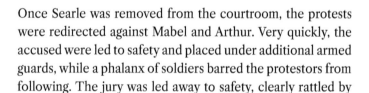

Once Searle was removed from the courtroom, the protests were redirected against Mabel and Arthur. Very quickly, the accused were led to safety and placed under additional armed guards, while a phalanx of soldiers barred the protestors from following. The jury was led away to safety, clearly rattled by the whole experience.

Frederick appealed for calm, and now denied a clear focus for their anger, an uneasy silence fell over the mob.

"You're proving his point," he began, and a chorus of jeers replied. "Taking matters into your own hands is not justice," he continued. "The purpose of this trial is to determine the facts of the matter at hand, and a robust defence is not only required but essential for justice to prevail. We might well hear things we do not like, but if they are pertinent to a defence, we must consent to hear them."

Rumblings continued among those gathered, but Frederick continued over the top of the murmuring.

"I will decide if such arguments are beyond the pale, not you. The jury will decide if they carry any weight, not you. If any of you have a guilty conscience about how you arrived in safety when so many others did not, then that is a matter you will need to address on your own. I will not have this courtroom disrupted by a gathering of those too fragile to hear a dissenting or uncomfortable opinion."

"You would let him insult us? Accuse us of the same crimes as these traitors?" a voice called from the back.

"I will let him make his point, and I will let Wharton refute it. That is how this will work. If you are unable to accept this, I will gladly exclude you from the proceedings. You can read those arguments in the transcript, after the fact. Or you can take up the position that you were so fortunate to have won and observe. The choice is yours, ladies and gentlemen."

The threat of being excluded from the trial, and having it completed behind closed doors, seemed to get through to the assembled people in a way that the logic of my brother's arguments had not. As Frederick tells it, at that moment he felt like a headmaster with a dozen naughty boys in front of him, shuffling their feet and looking anywhere but at him. "If it had not been so tense a situation, I would have laughed out loud," he later told me.

Suitably mollified, the observers were told that the trial would continue the next morning.

"Any additional outbursts like those today, even from those not in your number, will have the same result. Spread the word," Frederick told them, "and make sure we do not see behaviour like this again."

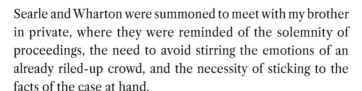

Searle and Wharton were summoned to meet with my brother in private, where they were reminded of the solemnity of proceedings, the need to avoid stirring the emotions of an already riled-up crowd, and the necessity of sticking to the facts of the case at hand.

"I have told the observers that if they disrupt proceedings, they will be removed from the court. I will tell you both the same thing now." Both men began to protest, but fell silent as Frederick raised a hand. "I will not hesitate to declare a mistrial, if I deem it necessary," he said (although he later admitted to me privately that the prospect filled him with dread). "Select a new jury, new advocates, and do whatever it takes to ensure justice is done and done fairly. That means no appeals to emotion, no insulting of the public. Am I clear?"

The two men agreed, albeit resentfully, and Frederick continued.

"Facts, gentlemen, above all. If you have a legal argument to make, you will make it without hyperbole. In return, I shall ensure you are both heard, and heard clearly. Mr Searle, I understand your approach, and I cannot deny that we survived where many did not. Those losses weigh on us all, and there may come a time when we will answer for the decisions that were made on our behalf. You and I are stood here by the Grace of God, or good fortune, call it whatever you will. But I will not have it suggested that we wished for, or caused the deaths of, our fellow countrymen. Find another way to put the jury into the shoes of the defendants, if you must, but any incitement to riot will be dealt with. Am I still making myself clear?"

"Yes, your honour. I only wished..."

"Save your arguments for the courtroom, Mr Searle."

# Chapter Twenty

# Preparation

We had scheduled twice daily radio calls with home, at fixed times. This way, either end could send out radio operators and beam messages without drawing attention to the home bases. I drafted a brief message in consultation with Chambers, explaining the situation and asking for support for my decision. I then returned to my bed-space to encipher the message in privacy. Before our departure, I had been issued with a small codebook that Frederick had insisted was never to leave my person. At the time, I had wondered what secrets we might be keeping from our allies, but now I saw the sense in it. Having to rely on their radio operator to transmit the message would have left our negotiations wide open to interception, and while I was certain that the reply from the government would be to agree to Armand's demands, in the unlikely event that they proposed a different course of action, it would be best if we were the only ones aware of it.

The reply came with such haste—almost immediately upon receipt of the request, when encryption times were taken into account—that the situation must have been anticipated and prepared for. The enciphered note was handed to me, and once again, I sought privacy for the transcoding process. Upon my emergence, Chambers could tell at a glance that the word from on high was that we were to cooperate, just by noticing the tension in my jaw.

"Why didn't they just tell us before we left?" I wondered aloud. "Clearly, they have no compunction about handing over our secrets and sharing the spoils, so why the charade of a consultation? Why even send me to be a negotiator, if there is to be no negotiation?"

"To make the Canadians think that they have won a greater victory," Chambers explained. "If we had merely acceded immediately, then they might have asked for more. If we give the impression of having to check with our superiors, then the request must have been much larger than we anticipated, and they know not to push further."

"But they would know that we got agreement instantly, would that not undermine the charade?" Amy asked.

"Welcome to politics," Chambers shrugged, and we went to tell Armand of the decision.

With an agreement reached, relations between ourselves and our hosts were cordial once more, if still strained. The face-saving manoeuvres of diplomacy had been accepted, though I was sure that no-one was fooled. In any case, we were ready to proceed.

The plan was simple once we got past Armand's love of dramatically revealing the details piece by piece. Men mined the ore, pushed it around the site in mine-carts on rails, and loaded it into the refinery mechanism. Some time later, this disgorged the now concentrated uranium into barrels of the strange Martian metal, which were capped off and loaded into the waiting truck. The depleted ore was ejected as a fine powder, which coated everything within the mining area with a thick grey layer of dust.

"It's unclear whether this dust or the radiation are the biggest risks to the men," Armand said. "Our sources say it's so fine as to get into and under the skin and coat the lungs. From a distance you cannot see the entrance into the mines, it floats about like smoke."

"So, how do you know all this?" I asked. "And for that matter, doesn't the mining take place below ground? It must all be invisible."

"We have agents who have infiltrated the place," Armand said. "They take their place each day, slave away while taking mental notes of anything that might be of use to us. Then we meet them after, and exchange notes."

"So they're aiding the Martians too?" Chambers sounded perturbed.

"Only as far as is necessary. And since we're stealing the spoils of their labour, they're helping us even beyond the information we need."

"Even so, could they not sabotage something? Destroy the refinery machine, or smuggle explosives into the mine?"

"The refinery is operated by a Martian, so there's no means to slip anything inside to damage it. Explosives in the mine would only kill men, and the Martians would replace them in an instant."

Chambers would not let go of his idea. "So kill the operator, then, there must be something."

Armand sighed. "They would replace him, too. But let's assume we could drive them away. What if we could not figure out the operation of the machine ourselves? Or we damaged it in the fighting? Then our supply of uranium is gone, and we have invited reprisals, all to no net benefit. I do not know how you run your resistance in England, but we have weighed up all our options and chosen the least offensive one. If you disagree, you may hold your tongue or return home."

Chambers, abashed, indicated Armand should continue.

"The barrels are lashed into the truck, and then two men drive it to the Martian base. Obviously, the route is overseen by the Martians; while they may not wish to transport the dangerous materials themselves, they also do not wish to let it out of their sight. One tripod always accompanies the vehicle, which they believe is what has prevented us from taking any action against it."

"So what has changed?" I asked.

"Your request meant that we had a reason to try. With so long without an attack, we're hoping they're complacent, and not watching exceptionally closely."

"You expect them not to notice?" Chambers scoffed. "I trust that is not the beginning and end of your plan!"

"Naturally not," Armand said. "Look at the route." He indicated a road on the map we had seen earlier. "From the mines, here, it passes through this canyon. Then it winds its way up the mountain side…"

"And into a tunnel!" I exclaimed as I recognised the symbol on the map. "It must be a half-mile long, at least!"

Armand appeared more irritated that I had guessed his plan than he had been at Chambers' nay-saying. "Nearly three-quarters, in fact."

I was excited to have worked out what I thought the whole idea was, but felt Amy's hand on my arm restraining me. I sat back and let Armand continue.

"So we have a part of the route where the truck is out of sight, and if the Martians wanted to investigate, they would find it hard to do so. Their fighting machines also won't fit in that tunnel, so it gives us our opportunity."

My impatience overcame me. "But you can't unload the uranium in the time it would take a truck to pass, not even with lifting equipment. And merely stealing the truck won't help you, since the Martians will just follow it when it comes out of the tunnel."

"Indeed," Armand smiled again. "But if a truck leaves the tunnel exactly when they expect..."

"A second truck," I exclaimed, "identical to the first, but empty."

"Loaded with rocks, it needs to move the same way, but yes. And once the Martian has escorted it out of sight, we drive the first one out and bring it here."

Even Chambers had to admit it was a good idea.

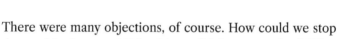

There were many objections, of course. How could we stop the truck in the tunnel if the drivers didn't want to obey? What if they raised the alarm somehow, or signalled the Martians that something was wrong? Armand had answers for all of these, truly he and his team had considered every place where the plan might come apart. One potential issue, however, gave him pause.

"What if they can detect the radiation?" I asked. "If they see the decoy truck leave but sense there is no uranium in the back, they'll know instantly that something is amiss."

"We are assuming that they cannot, or do not, check," he admitted. "It's possible that the barrels, being made of their own alloys, block enough radiation as to make it all but undetectable."

"If that were so, they wouldn't run the risk of having men transport it," Chambers pointed out. "There must be leakage enough for them to be afraid of it, which means there would be enough to detect."

"Can we fake that signal somehow?" Amy asked. "Take some of the uranium from the first truck and place it, un-shielded, in the second?"

"Too dangerous," Armand said. "Not to mention we wouldn't have time."

"Or one of your agents could sneak some of the ore out, then."

"We would have to match the radiation level, and without the right apparatus to detect and quantify that we'd never stand a chance. We'll have to trust to providence; we'll know soon enough. The moment the decoy truck emerges, the Martian will let us know if we are rumbled."

"What happens then?" I asked. Armand's only reply was a grimace.

The assault was planned for the following morning. Armand's agents had been tracking the amount of uranium refined so far, and their estimates suggested that the truck would depart at around eight a.m. This would place it in the tunnel by a little after nine o'clock, by which time our decoy would need to be in position and our forces ready to intercept.

"So soon?" Amy asked. "It is good we arrived when we did."

Armand smiled. "If you had not, we would have delayed until the next shipment, but that would be a week or more. Why wait?"

That only left the question of who was to go on the mission. Armand naturally would be leading it, and Chambers nominated himself as England's representative. Whether he believed Armand might try to swindle us, or merely wanted to oversee things out of curiosity or a sense of duty, he did not let on.

Amy assumed that they would not find a place for a woman, and having no desire to take part in any case, quickly ruled herself out of the plans.

"But my husband will do a fine job in my stead," she announced, to my surprise. I had assumed that once again she would entreat me not to place myself in harm's way. Even so, I expected Armand to refuse, saying that there was no room for a writer and chronicler on the mission, when he had the need of men who could fight if the need arose.

But I had forgotten that I had never been introduced to him as a writer, merely as a part of the British contingent. For all he knew, I was Chambers' right hand man, and fully deserving of a place. Or perhaps he knew of my account of the first invasion after all and flattered himself that I would sing of his heroic achievements when all this was over. In either case, I was granted a place.

To my surprise, Armand also insisted that Amy would be welcome to join us, if she so desired. With a sinking heart, I saw the gleam in her eyes and knew I could not persuade her to stay behind.

## Chapter Twenty-One

# Attack

In bed that night, I whispered to Amy. "Why did you nominate me?"

"You would have begged me to let you go, would you not?"

"It would be foolish to come all this way and not witness the turning point of our resistance," I admitted. "But I expected you to talk me out of it, as you did before."

"And you went anyway, despite my protests," she said. "Then once again, when I was captured."

"I promised you no more heroics," I pointed out. "And I assumed you would not embark on any either."

"How else can I ensure you keep your promise?" she chuckled.

"This is no job for a woman," I protested. "As capable as you have proven yourself to be," I hastily added.

"I refuse to sit here, wringing my hands while I wait for news of my husband. If it is safe enough for you to go, then it will be safe enough for me. Besides, I do not believe riding in a truck and outwitting a Martian counts as heroic." She laughed quietly. "Brave, perhaps. Noble, certainly. But this plan involves no fighting, no daring escapes. I think we are going to be well able to keep our promises of utter cowardice."

I kissed her goodnight, and fell into an uneasy sleep, full of dreams of stalking Martian war machines.

We were awoken at six, ate a hasty breakfast, and returned to our rooms. We dressed in silence, pulling on our borrowed cold-weather clothing.

As we clambered aboard the truck, I noticed in the lamp-light that it had been repainted since we had been collected at the docks, presumably to better resemble the one used by the transport vehicle. My lack of rest caught up with me, and I confess that despite the excitement of the morning's activities I nodded off a few times in the rear of the vehicle, only to be jolted awake as we ran into another of the potholes that seemed to make up a large proportion of the roads in Canada.

By a little after eight, we were in position inside the tunnel. Armand placed the truck at the mid-point, angled across the road to form a blockage. This far north, at this time of year, the sky was still pitch black, but Armand assured me that even when dawn came, the dark of the tunnel would render the vehicle all but invisible. When viewed from the daylight outside, it was impossible to tell that the road was impeded. By the time the delivery drivers would see us, they would be out of sight of the Martian chaperoning them.

"With luck, the truck will be driven by our men anyway," Armand said, "but we're not relying on luck. If we should have to restrain someone, we are prepared to."

"Without injuring them, I would hope," I said. "Whether these men are pressed into service or not, I am not comfort-able killing."

"That will be up to them," Armand said. "When we offer them sanctuary with us, and an end to their travails, I suspect any resistance will melt away quite rapidly."

"Can they be trusted?" Chambers asked. "If they've collaborated, how can you be sure they won't betray you?"

"We cannot, but we hope that they will join us. And until we can be certain, we will take precautions, of course."

We settled in for a long wait, guards watching the entrance and exit of our hiding place carefully. Dawn came, eerie without the accompanying chorus of birdsong. My stomach rumbled, reminding me that breakfast had been some time ago by now. Provisions were passed around, the guards were changed, and suitably refreshed, we resumed our vigil.

There was a short spell of silence before Amy asked a question. "Who will drive the decoy truck? Some of your men, evidently. You won't risk a collaborator raising the alarm."

"Exactly," Armand said. "If our drivers bring the uranium in, they will drive the decoy out. If not, Hannam and Wright there will do it." He gestured at two men in soiled coveralls. "You need not worry about us being betrayed."

"That is not why I asked," she explained. "I was wondering what might happen when the truck reaches its destination."

I was about to comment that while it would be a shame not to see the Martian's consternation when they realised they had been robbed, when I realised the true thrust of her question. "What happens to the drivers, you mean?"

"Precisely. Even if there was a chance of the Martians understanding their pleas for mercy, they would not be inclined to grant them." She lowered her voice and leaned in towards us. "Those men are going to their deaths."

Armand nodded. "You need not lower your voice, they know precisely what awaits them."

"Is there no way to rescue them?" I asked, even though I knew the answer.

"After they have arrived, no. And snatching them from the truck, while en route under the noses of the Martians, would only result in more deaths."

"So they abandon the truck, run for it," I said.

"That would raise the alarm too early," Armand said. "And set the Martians on our tail before we reached safety. Believe me, we have considered all the possibilities."

The death of these men, volunteers as they may be, did not sit well with me. Any other protests would have to wait, though, as the guard at the entrance gave the signal that we had been awaiting.

---

Three long blasts on a whistle echoed through the tunnel, indicating the truck had been spotted.

"Places, men!" Armand called. "And woman," he added with a nod at Amy. Chambers, Amy and I had no active roles to play, and so our orders were to keep hidden. If bullets did start flying, we ought to be safe behind the decoy truck.

As the rumbling diesel engine of the uranium delivery vehicle approached, I realised too late that if the driver intended to ram the roadblock, we would be crushed beneath the decoy before we could react. Fortunately, the engine slowed, and the brakes squealed. I risked a peek over the bonnet.

Four of Armand's men had levelled rifles at the cab of the newly arrived truck, and Armand himself was waving for the men to get out. They were clearly not his own men, then. As they clambered down from the cab, they raised their hands in surrender, and were directed to kneel against the tunnel wall where they were kept at gunpoint.

Hannam and Wright climbed swiftly into the cab of the decoy truck, and with a nod to Armand, gunned the engine and drove it along the tunnel. We stood aside to let them pass, and a tear sprang to my eye at the sign of such quiet bravery. In moments, the truck left the safety of the tunnel and entered the light. I watched until it rounded the bend, and I could sense the tension in the tunnel lifting.

The drivers had welcomed their liberation with gratitude, and now that I had a chance to regard them closely, I could see why. They wore the same filthy overalls as the decoys, though even more tattered and grimy. The fabric hung from them as if on a clothes-hanger, so thin were these men. Their faces were sunken, hollow-cheeked, and beneath the dirt they had a yellowish hue. Thin, patchy stubble covered their cheeks, and their hair was lank and thinning. I shuddered at the reminder of what radiation could do to a man and wondered if they would indeed live any longer in liberty than they would have in servitude.

As we were climbing aboard our prize, the ground rumbled beneath us. Everyone looked around in confusion until the lookout at the tunnel exit raised the alarm.

"Fire!" he shouted. Sure enough, greasy black smoke was rising from a point along the road, and I could only imagine the cause.

Armand swore loudly. "They spotted the switch," he said. "We move, now!" he yelled, and all hands sprang into action. The sickly men were loaded aboard the truck, and we took our place next to them, nestled among the uranium canisters.

The truck sprang into life and lurched towards the entrance to the tunnel, back in the direction from which it had come.

"Would it not be better to stay hidden?" I wondered aloud.

"We'd be pinned down," Chambers pointed out. "At least this way we stand a chance."

We burst out of the tunnel, and light flooded the interior of the truck. What I had been calling barrels were revealed to be triangular in cross-section, like prisms. They lay on the bed of the truck along one of their flat sides, and were lashed down with canvas straps to avoid them moving. Each of us was shying away from them as much as we could, as if an extra inch or two of separation would protect us from the fires within. Logically, I knew the greater danger was outside, that the pursuing Martians would be much more likely to spell our doom, but there is something insidious about an unseen danger that concentrates the mind in a peculiar fashion.

"Let's hope they do not wish to risk their cargo," Amy said. For a moment I thought she meant Armand, that he would not take risks in driving us. Then I realised she meant that the Martians might pull their punches to be able to retrieve what we had stolen. I looked at the canisters again, would they survive a blast from the heat-ray? If so, they might simply burn us to a crisp and retrieve their property at their leisure.

All these thoughts flashed through my mind in an instant. The idea of an unseen danger refused to leave me, and I felt strangely compelled to see our adversary if I could. I crawled on hands and knees to the back of the truck, despite Amy's pleas to remain seated, and poked my head out.

Trees and bushes, wrapped in their blanket of red weed, flashed by on either side. The canyon walls rose behind them, ensuring we could not depart from the road even if we wished to. Should we have gone the other way? No, I reasoned, we knew for sure that there was a Martian there, who had destroyed the decoy. The road might also be blocked by the debris. This way was probably also guarded, but it offered us the only chance of escape. I craned my neck, looking upwards to the very tops of the cliffs that hemmed us in, and saw a glint of metal.

"Martian!" I called, and a series of voices relayed the cry to Armand in the driving seat. "Atop the right hand cliff!"

"Let me know if he moves," came the reply.

The juddering movement of the truck made precise observations difficult, but I strained my eyes to make out details. I could not see a projector, at any rate. "No sign of a heat-ray yet," I shouted. Then something moved, was it a tentacle? "Hold on," I called. Then I saw it. "Black smoke!"

The smoke coiled down the cliff-side, a few hundred yards behind us. Thick and oily, it moved deceptively fast, reaching the canyon floor in seconds. Like a living being, it pursued us, gaining on us all too quickly. "It's catching us!" I shouted. "Hurry up!" As if Armand wasn't already driving as fast as he dared, if not faster, the truck's wheels protesting at every small bend in the road.

As the cloud of death neared us, I retreated back inside the truck, falling into place beside Amy and wrapping my arms around her. I had no words, nothing I could say at these final moments, apart from these.

"I love you," I whispered.

Before she could form any reply, the truck lurched hard to the left. A loud bang reverberated through the vehicle as we hit something, and the rear corner sprang into the air. The barrels did not shift, but the people inside flew about as though robbed of their weight. When the wheel slammed back into the road, we landed awkwardly sprawled on the floor, a tangle of arms and legs. Still, our headlong escape continued, and I glanced back towards the rear of the truck bed once more. The smoke was more distant, only slightly, but enough. I realised we were climbing, ascending a slope. We must have turned off the main road and begun climbing the valley wall. The truck slowed as the engine strained, but the smoke was falling further and further behind us, unable to fill the entire valley and rise to meet us. I breathed a sigh of relief, and released Amy from the bear-hug I had enclosed her in.

"I love you too," she said when her breath returned.

# Chapter Twenty-Two

# Escape

By sheer providence, the road which ascended the slope of the ravine was on the opposite side to the Martian fighting machine. I watched from the rear of the truck as it put away the black smoke emitter and retrieved the projector for the heat-ray instead. Surely we were too far for it to have any meaningful effect? Nevertheless...

"Get down!" I called, and everyone lay flat on the truck's bed. Light illuminated the interior, but the loading flap of the lorry protected us from direct exposure. As it had done aboard the ship, our distance had protected us, as the canvas covering the truck did not smoulder or burn. One foolhardy man poked his head up over the rear and immediately cried out in alarm. He clutched his eyes and fell back among us, but did not scream. Amy was at his side in an instant and quickly determined that he could no longer see a thing. His shout had been of surprise, rather than pain, for there are no pain-sensing nerves in the rear of our eyes to warn us when the retina is burned away.

If any other among us had needed additional warnings to stay out of sight, this would have served. After a few moments, the light vanished once more, and I judged that the Martian had realised the futility of his attack. For a terrifying instant, I remembered the extensible legs on the machine that had pursued us at sea. Could it step across the ravine and overtake us? I had to know, but did not dare to peek out of the rear of our transport and risk instant blindness, or worse, if the machine had indeed made it closer. When no repeat of the blinding light came, and no sizzle of burning canvas, I had to assume that the Martian was unable to pursue us. The lorry reached the top of the incline, gathered speed, and we barrelled down the other side of the hill at breakneck speed.

Despite grabbing on to any surface that might provide support, every bend in the road flung us around like cards in a tombola. I wedged myself between one side of the lorry and one of the uranium containers, glad that they were well strapped down and hoping that indeed they were thick enough to protect me. Perhaps pursuit was coming, maybe another Martian had been stationed on this side of the ravine after all, and was chasing us down at that very moment. I hammered on the back of the lorry's cab to get the driver's attention.

Almost immediately, the lorry slowed, as if I had reminded our driver of his delicate cargo. We were able to release our vice-like grip and position ourselves a little more comfortably. Shortly afterwards, the lorry slowed and swung to the left before coming to a careful halt. I was poking my head out of the back to see what was happening when Armand came around to check on us.

"Any injuries?" he asked bluntly.

Amy indicated her blinded ward, and a few of our companions complained of cuts and bruises. One sprained ankle needed dressing, and a few ribs were suspected to be broken, but all in all, we had come out of the chase in remarkably good condition.

"Why the headlong dash?" I asked Armand. "Were we pursued out of the valley?"

He shrugged. "When we saw the heat-ray projector, we smashed off the mirrors so it couldn't blind us. That worked, but then we had no way of knowing what was back there. Jenkins kept his foot down until your banging made us look for somewhere to stop. We shouldn't wait here though, they'll be looking for us."

With the immediate medical needs of our passengers dealt with, the journey resumed.

The panic and fear of the narrow escape abated quickly, leaving us all as exhausted as if we had fled the Martian danger on foot. The nearness of our doom and the deaths of the decoy drivers cast a pall over us, and one man uttered a whispered prayer for the lost souls, crossing himself fervently.

With time to dwell on our situation, my mind ran away from me as it was wont to do. Once again, I had endangered my life, but this time I had also imperilled my beloved Amy. No doubt she would protest that her presence had been her own decision, and that I should face none of the blame. Nevertheless, I could not excuse myself for failing in what I saw as my duty. When this was over, I resolved we would remain safe, hidden in Salisbury and I would assist my brother with the day-to-day running of the base. Perhaps, in time, we might play a part in the rebuilding of our civilisation, but until that day came, our place was not here on the front lines of a battle that had all but destroyed our world.

I turned to Amy to inform her of my decision, only to find her peering intently out of the rear of the lorry. I followed her gaze, but could see nothing.

"What is it?" I asked her.

"I'm not sure," she replied. "Something following us, perhaps. Or it might be nothing. I don't wish to raise the alarm until I am sure."

"Martian?" I said quietly.

She shook her head. "Not one of their machines, it's too small and looked alive. Probably a bear or something, we shall leave it behind soon enough." She continued her careful observations, and I leaned forward to get a better view for myself. The idea of seeing a bear in the wild, never having seen one outside of the London Zoo, enticed me. That's when I saw it.

"There!" I called, and pointed. "Is that what you saw?"

"Yes! What is it, though?"

I could not be certain of what it was. In overgrown terrain, uneven lighting and while being jostled around in the back of a lorry, it was difficult to make out anything other than a vague impression. It was large, slow-moving, and a dark reddish brown in colour. Its lower half was hidden behind the undergrowth, and I could not even be sure which end was the head. Something about it disturbed me, however, though I could not place what caused me such disquiet. As it disappeared into the distance behind us, I was glad to see it go.

"Another!" Amy called, and pointed. This one was closer to the side of the road, and as we watched, it moved out onto the clear ground behind us, giving us our first clear look at it.

It was a Martian.

Outside of its fighting machine, crawling laboriously over the ground, it was strangely less intimidating than I might have expected. I recalled the first one I had seen, struggling in the pit on Horsell Common. This one looked less agile even than that, as though it had been dragging itself along for days on end. What on earth was it doing, unsupported by any means of transport?

Amy was hammering on the lorry's cab again, and it swiftly slowed to a halt. The men alongside us dashed from the truck and took up positions to either side of the vehicle, rifles trained unwaveringly on the creature about a hundred yards away. Armand rounded the truck to investigate the commotion and stopped in his tracks when he saw the Martian.

"What the devil...?" he gasped.

"It might not be the only one," I said, and informed him of the creature we had taken to be a bear.

"But why?" Armand asked. "If they were scouting, they'd be in their tripods, or some other vehicle—we've seen a few wheeled transports from time to time—so why risk being out in the open and so vulnerable to attack?"

"Not just attack," Amy said. "Their machines offer them protection from bacteria and virus. I can't think why they'd expose themselves like this."

"Perhaps they did not choose to," I said. I felt all eyes upon me, and with a gulp, I pressed on. "What if they were cast out?"

"A punishment?" Armand mused. "Possibly, though a very cruel and ultimately fatal one. What transgression would warrant such a fate?"

"Who knows how their minds work," I said. "Perhaps theft, murder, or mutiny. But I wonder if it might not be another reason."

"They're sick," Amy said. "I mean, they got sick and so they were exiled to avoid infecting the others."

We looked at the creature, and I confess for one fleeting moment I felt a small measure of pity for it. To be cast out of your home, sentenced to death on a foreign shore, must have been terrifying. I considered the leper colonies of our own world, where sufferers were isolated to avoid contaminating the rest of society. But at least they received treatment, such as was possible; the Martian had been left to fend for itself and would surely die. Such a reminder of our different natures merely reinforced how alien these creatures truly were.

"Russell was right, then," I said. "Their defences are flawed after all. Some disease can get through."

"What do we do?" Amy asked.

# Chapter Twenty-Three

# Martian

"Kill it." Armand spoke quietly, and the man beside him lifted his rifle to obey.

"Wait!" Amy called. Everyone turned to look, startled by her outburst. "The sound," she explained. "If they are still searching for us, they will hear the rifle-shot."

"I'm not going over there with a knife," the rifleman said. "No fear."

The thing's tentacles still thrashed around as it attempted to escape us. While not as ferocious or as strong as the handling equipment in the tripods, they could still snatch a man up, drag him away or choke him, as I had seen.

"Leave it then," Armand said. "It'll die soon enough."

"Should we not capture it?" I asked. Now it was my turn to wither under the stares of all around me. "Might it not prove useful?"

Armand laughed. "Be my guest," he said, with a bow towards the creature. "Perhaps it will come quietly, but I think you might have to restrain it." His men laughed along with him, and I wilted still further.

"Some insight might come from it," I protested. "Alright, we cannot interrogate it, but some scientific investigation could prove fruitful."

No laughter greeted this suggestion, at least. I looked to Chambers for support.

"It's sick," he agreed. "Which means that whatever means they have been using to protect themselves has failed." He paused for a moment, deep in thought. "It might be that his machine sprang a leak, allowed in the air and he became infected. But they have treatments, so that must imply he has contracted some strain that defeats their medicine. If so, we cannot pass up this opportunity."

"I'm not going over there," the rifleman said again. Armand assured him that he wouldn't have to.

"If our visitors think it is so important, then they shall be happy to oblige, I'm sure." Again, he bowed theatrically.

Chambers and I exchanged a look, and Amy grasped my arm. I bent slightly, and she whispered in my ear.

"You can't be serious," she said. "Even weakened, it could still kill you. Not to mention whatever disease it has might have come from one of their prisoners, and could also infect you."

"If you're willing to explain to Russell why we left this opportunity unused, then I will climb back into the lorry and we can head home. But this is a rare, possibly unique chance to learn something which will be vital. You know he's not going to admit whether his plague researches are going well or not, and we shouldn't leave any stone unturned."

"At least let me do it," she urged. "I have medical experience, after all."

"Chambers and I will do it," I declared. "If there are to be any injuries, we will need you to dress our wounds."

Reluctantly, she agreed with my assessment. Under the impatient stare of Armand, we formulated a plan.

Amy would distract the Martian, flapping a blanket as a mata-
dor to a bull, in the hopes that it would not notice Chambers
and me for as long as possible. She positioned herself directly
in front of it, at a safe distance from its reach, and began
waving the cloth as enticingly as possible. It struggled towards
her slowly, hauling its flabby body over the rough ground in a
way that must have been agonising. On its home planet, with
a third of its weight here, the stones might not feel as sharp;
but here it must have felt like crawling over broken glass.

Chambers and I split up, one to each side, and walked away
at a right angle, monitoring its attention all the way. A few
dozen yards away, we were confident that its attention was focused on my wife, and we circled around behind it. Chambers
was brandishing an empty syringe from the medical supply
kit the lorry carried, while I clutched a hatchet in my white
knuckled grip. If the creature should turn toward us, or try to
grab either of us, I would use it to deter or sever any tentacle
that threatened us. I would have felt happier having a rifle
trained on the thing, but as Amy had already closed down
that approach, Armand had sent his soldiers to work patrolling
around us to avoid a surprise attack, which they had done with
barely disguised resentment. It was a better use of our limited
weaponry, I had to admit.

Chambers and I rendezvoused at the rear of the Martian
and together crept towards it. I saw Armand stifle a smile as
we tip-toed forward, afraid of making a sound that might alert
it to our presence. I tried to remember what little I knew of
the anatomy of these things. They could hear, after a fashion,
though having evolved in a thinner atmosphere, it was difficult
to be sure how acute their hearing would be on Earth. Despite
the blood thudding in my own ears, I endeavoured to commit
every aspect of our approach to memory—there would be a

great deal to learn from this encounter beyond the samples I would take.

Eventually we were within an arm's reach of the leathery carapace. The Martian was almost as tall as I, and just as wide. From behind it appeared almost spherical, though it was longer front-to-back. The tentacles emerged from its front end, by which it was hauling itself slowly forward towards my wife, though I knew it could reach all around itself with them if it needed. A smaller ring of similar manipulators ringed the triangular mouth, thankfully invisible from where I stood, although I could hear them wetly flicking back and forth. The creature still struggled forward, Amy slowly stepping back-wards as it neared. She continued to wave the blanket, but gave us a small nod to signal that she had the Martian's full attention.

Chambers uncapped the needle, took a deep breath, and stepped forward the last few feet. The stink of the creature filled my nostrils, a sickening blend of metal and gunpowder I thought, and its wheezing breath stank of death. He picked the spot, aimed the needle, and slammed it into the back of the struggling beast.

It let out a deafening cry, quite taking us all by surprise. Amy tripped over in her retreat and dropped the blanket. A tentacle shot out towards her, lightning fast, but came up short. Chambers lost his grip on the syringe, but fortunately it remained deeply implanted in the Martian's skin, poking upwards like a planted flag. Chambers had let out a small shriek at the sound, and now clamped his hand over his mouth, embarrassed at his outburst.

He regained his composure, grasped the syringe, and began pulling back the plunger. Nothing happened, no blood filled the glass. He yanked out the needle and tried again, to another yelp from the beast. Still, nothing came. As he pulled the needle free again, I saw a tentacle writhing towards us as the Martian tried to grasp whatever was hurting it. I lunged in and swung the hatchet. I missed, striking the beast's back instead. I stepped back a pace, watching the flicking of the tentacle over the spots I had struck, probing the injuries. Readying the axe once more, I swung hard, and this time my aim was true. The tip of the tentacle was sliced clean off, and the force of the blow carried the hatchet into the flesh of the Martian's carapace, splitting it open. The tentacle writhed in evident agony, and the wail that emitted from the creature's mouth was twice as loud as before. We could only pray that any Martian overhearing the battle would assume it was the dying sounds of their diseased comrade, and refuse to investigate.

Blood pooled around the axe-head, still lodged in place. Chambers hurried forward, plunged the needle into the gash, and drew up a syringe full of the toxic-looking liquid. The tentacle still flailed about wildly, and I tried to intercept it from striking my compatriot, although it was clearly moving without any controlled purpose. Blood jetted from the severed end, and I felt it splashing hot against my skin and clothes. The smell, already unpleasant, became unbearable, and I completed my task and withdrew before I vomited.

We regrouped a safe distance from the Martian, Chambers holding the syringe and its precious contents, and I carrying the severed length of the tentacle as a trophy. Amy used the blanket to wipe the worst of the blood off us, and we climbed back into the lorry. Chambers wrapped the syringe in a bandage from the first aid kit to protect the fragile glass from further bumps in the road, while I used another length of crepe to stanch the bleeding of the almost eight inches of tentacle that I had recovered. Both were placed into the emptied out medical box and I cradled it on my lap.

Our prizes safely stowed, Armand blew a whistle to regroup his men, and we set off once more, the rest of the company sitting as far from Chambers and I, and our stink, as they could manage in the confined space.

Chapter Twenty-Four

# Return

We saw no more Martians on our journey back to the base, other than one fighting machine in the far distance. Chambers wondered whether our route through their 'leper colony' had dissuaded them from following us, while Amy believed that we had merely outmanoeuvred them and shaken off their pursuit. My own thoughts were somewhat distracted.

I have long been a hypochondriac, each ache or pain setting me wondering what fresh ailment I had developed. As a child, I had often been quite sick, collecting the diseases common to children one after another. Mumps, chicken pox, and a brush with measles had left me wary of contagion, but it was a long-lived episode of whooping cough that stuck in my memory as the most terrifying. My recovery had been slow, necessitating an extended stay out of the smog of London with a distant relative before I was pronounced as fully convalesced. Even so, the coughs and sneezes all around that heralded the arrival of winter filled me with a peculiar dread, my mind unwilling to accept that those long days of gasping and wheezing were behind me.

So when I began to feel chilled on the way back, I was certain that I had contracted whatever ailment had afflicted the Martian, perhaps by the splashes of its blood, or by the droplets in its struggling breaths. With difficulty, I was able to convince myself that it was merely my mind playing tricks.

Any sickness would have to take time to develop, there was none that could take hold within minutes, or even hours. My shivering was merely an after-effect of the shock, I reasoned, not to mention the breeze through the lorry that was keeping the stench at bearable levels. I pulled the blanket tighter around myself and tried to put all ideas of illness from my mind. Chambers, for his part, seemed unaffected by the ordeal, and I took solace in the idea that if I was indeed sick, he would also have been showing signs or symptoms.

Nonetheless, my active imagination would give me no respite until we arrived back at the base, certain that we had not been followed. We filed inside, in high spirits at the success of our mission, and revelled in the applause and cheers of the folks who had remained behind.

Armand soaked up the adulation, something which I did not begrudge him. He had put together this entire plan, recruited the soldiers, and carried it out. We could so easily have returned empty-handed, or not at all, and a celebration was undeniably deserved.

As was a hot bath. There might have been plenty of water, but heating large volumes was still a challenge. As such, there was not sufficient for Chambers and me to clean ourselves of the now dried Martian blood by bathing in the usual manner. We had buckets of hot water provided, but we were required to sponge ourselves off in a standing position rather than soak in a tub. The cloth I used was quite black by the time I felt my skin sufficiently scoured, and the water in the first bucket was a filthy greenish-grey. I splashed water from the second to rinse away the last evidence of the day's horrors, before upending the entire vessel over my head and watching the water sink gurgling between the cracks in the stone floor.

A clean, if not exactly soft, towel wrapped around me, I went in search of fresh clothing.

Once dressed, I realised how long it had been since my last meal. With the fear and tension of the day ebbing at last, my body was crying out for sustenance. Amy had left a note informing me that she was already in the mess hall, and I made haste to join her.

Armand was sat at the head table, the soldiers from the mission arrayed alongside him like a scene from the Last Supper. Perhaps he could take the adoration too far, I mused, before putting any such fears aside and digging in to the food laid out in front of me. Chambers had joined Amy already, and they were demolishing their own plates of food with evident delight. I ate so much, and so fast, that by the time I stopped I was over-filled to the point of sleepiness. Any fears of infection had gone; apart from a little drowsiness, I now felt as good as I had in days. The burble of conversation on all sides was lulling me into sleep, when with a start I remembered our prize.

"The blood!" I cried, sitting bolt upright.

Amy placed her hand on my arm. "Safe," she said. "Armand has placed it and the severed tentacle in the coolest cave they have to preserve them."

"Might he not be plotting to keep them?" I whispered. "He was reluctant to hand over the uranium without concessions, what might he ask for these rewards?"

"I am sure that he views them as your property," Amy replied, "since you and Chambers were the ones to gather them. In any case, that sounds like a problem for tomorrow."

My eyelids were so heavy I lacked the will to protest, and Amy and I went to bed where I slept the instant my head hit the straw-packed pillow.

———◄O►———

As I had feared, Armand was not keen to relinquish his claim on the spoils. "The same deal as the uranium," he said. "Split in half."

"You said it was a waste of time," Chambers protested. "And made us do the work. We risked our lives, were covered in blood, and now you claim half?"

"Need I remind you that we planned the mission, took you on it, risked our own lives and, indeed, sacrificed two good men? We are trusting your good will to share the results of your analysis with us. If we can perform our own tests, we can verify your research, and perhaps each team can spot something the other might overlook."

I was glad Russell wasn't here to overhear this slight against his abilities, though I had to concede Armand made a good point. Now the challenge was to convince Chambers to back down. I cast an imploring look at Amy, but she merely nodded back at me. Her faith in my diplomatic skills was touching, even as I was sure it was misplaced.

"I think we can agree it was a team effort to secure the sample," I said. "And continuing that teamwork would certainly be in all our interests. But we do have the better facilities in England, and a team already researching suitable pathogens. I'm sure you agree, Armand, that we are better placed to make the breakthrough we so desperately need. No disrespect to your own researchers, of course."

He nodded, slightly.

"So it would be disastrous if we ran short of material just as we reached the verge of a breakthrough, would it not?"

Another small nod.

"So perhaps a two-thirds share to our scientists, then?"

When Armand did not immediately refuse, but pondered the suggestion, I wondered if perhaps I had been selling myself short after all.

"Very well," Armand accepted. "And I believe we can provide some ice to protect your cargo."

Chambers stood open-mouthed at the speed of the resolution. I could see he was considering protesting that we should still take possession of the entire blood sample, but thought better of incurring Armand's displeasure. "What about the tentacle?" he asked cautiously.

"I doubt much will be learned from it, you might as well keep it as a trophy," Armand smiled. He signalled to one of his men, who brought a jar over to him. It looked like one of the jars Amy had preserved fruits in, back when we thought we might ride out a potential invasion in our home. Filled with a clear fluid, the severed end of the Martians' tentacle floated within, curling and writhing with the motion of the liquid in a most disconcerting manner.

"Formaldehyde?" I wondered aloud.

"Alcohol," Armand replied, tipping the jar from side to side and watching the movement of the severed appendage. "Well, mostly. We had a little trouble with moonshiners in the early days. We turn a blind eye to the small-scale brewers, but when drunkenness started to affect our chances of survival, we had to step in. Believe me, it's better used for this purpose than for drinking." He chuckled and passed the jar over to Chambers, who peered inside. "If there is nothing else, no doubt you wish to signal your ship and schedule your return?"

I could not help but feel that we had been summarily dismissed, and for a moment felt slighted by the way we had been cast aside once our usefulness ended. Then I realised that we had contributed little to the success of the mission, and were leaving with a couple of extremely valuable prizes. The suddenness of our departure might also be seen as a blessing; if the Martians had somehow tracked us back to the base, or could find it at any point in the future, we would be a long way from any reprisals.

Chapter Twenty-Five

# Boat

Our convoy set off before dawn two days later. Our share of the uranium occupied one lorry, while another carried supplies for the Minadora, as we had promised. Surprisingly, Armand had not protested handing over food to men he had never met, as seemingly they had enough to spare. Perhaps he just wanted us to leave on good terms, and filled with tales of his generosity. Or perhaps he had plans to forge a friendship with the ships's crew. He also had fresh water in abundance, and so a few barrels were tightly lashed down alongside the food supply. He had drawn the line at medicines, though—these were in such short supply that he hadn't even waited for us to ask before he informed us that this was not negotiable. We had assumed as much, but were able to put on a show of understanding disappointment at the news. My newly acquired political skills were being put to good use.

I was on edge the entire trip to the docks, certain that a Martian would ambush us, or a trio of fighting machines would chase us down to take back what was theirs. Had they not discovered our deception almost immediately? If they could track the radiation from the uranium, we were surely drawing targets on our backs, driving it across open country. Even when we pulled into the harbour area, I could not relax. I tried to convince myself that I was only apprehensive about the sea voyage again, that all would be well and my worst experience would be another round of sea-sickness, but while Chambers supervised the loading of the cargo onto the tenders that would take it to the Minadora, I scanned the horizon constantly. Every shadow cast by a passing cloud made me jump, and if there had still been birds in the sky, I would no doubt have startled at every one.

By the time the small boats were ready to go, I was quite exhausted and struggling under the burden of a headache. I was glad to sit down and allow someone else to row us out to the Minadora, and when the coastline and the threat it contained finally sank below the horizon, I let out a vast sigh.

Upon reaching our vessel, my headache was clearing up, and I was feeling a good deal better. I remarked upon this to Amy, merely out of curiosity at how the concerns of the mind can affect the body, but was startled when she revealed she also had been struck by headaches which had lifted once we got out to sea.

"I thought it was just me," Chambers said. A good number of the other men who had accompanied us also reported something similar.

"Might there be something in the air?" I asked. "Some malaise, some poison introduced by the Martians?" I shuddered at memories of the black smoke. I had seen nothing like that, but perhaps they had something more insidious.

"It felt as if I was underground again," one man said. "In those caves, you know?"

"Yeah," another piped up. "But not musty, or damp, just... close?"

Chambers' eyes widened. "Carbonic gas," he said. "I just bet it is."

"And what is that?" Amy asked, worriedly.

"The gas we exhale," Chambers said. "We inhale oxygen, and our bodies use that to convert our food into energy. The byproduct is also known as carbon dioxide, and too much of it can be dangerous."

"Are we safe?" I asked, my throat tightening even as I spoke.

"Quite," said Chambers. "It isn't toxic, as such, but too much causes lethargy, headaches, and eventually you will fall unconscious. I suspect there was a pocket of it at the docks; it's denser than regular air and so can gather at low points. Probably came from the decomposition of some old cargo, or something like that." His expression, however, did not suggest that he was satisfied with this deduction, and I resolved to speak to him later to determine the truth behind his concern.

The following morning, I asked Chambers what he was hiding. I was done with beating around the bush, hoping that the men in charge of operations would deign to tell me what I wanted to know, and had overnight resolved to take a more forceful approach. He insisted we head out on deck to discuss it.

"Less chance of being overheard," he explained, as we leaned on the railing, bundled up against the cold.

I looked over at the cabin-boy, keeping a discreet distance as always. "And what do you not wish to be heard?" I asked.

"Speculation, mostly. If I could be certain, I might be happier to discuss the matter, or if I thought there was something that could be done about it. There is no point in spreading mere supposition, and the panic or distrust that it would engender."

"The gas," I said. "Carbon dioxide, you said?"

He nodded. "I had feared it would be starting to build up by now. Russell first alerted me to the possibility, but with the excitement of the escape from Shropshire, then the mission here..."

"The possibility of what?" I said.

"Terraforming. Or Aresforming, if you prefer."

I recognised the roots of the words, but their meaning was opaque. "What do you mean?" I pressed.

"A vague scientific idea, at least so far, mere speculation. It's the idea of reshaping a world to make it more suited to its inhabitants. Some of the more inventive fiction writers have explored the idea of transforming a planet to make it habitable for us, seeding plants or microbes to produce the gases and foods we need to survive."

"The red weed." It made perfect sense. It hadn't stowed away, an unwanted passenger on the Martian cylinders, but had been brought deliberately.

"Precisely," Chambers confirmed. "Experiments in our labs showed that it produces an excess of carbon dioxide, depleting the oxygen in the atmosphere as part of the process."

I struggled to remember biology lessons from my school days. "But plants take in carbon, use it to build their leaves and stems. And the red weed grows so virulently, it must be absorbing even more than our own plants and trees do."

"In the growth phase, certainly, although it takes much of its mass from the soil. That's the mechanism that leaves the earth barren for almost anything else. Then once it reaches a critical size, it stops growing. You must have noticed?"

Now that the matter was pointed out to me, I realised that I had, although I had not realised the significance of the observation. The weed had spread wildly at first, and then stopped expanding its influence. While in the early days of the invasion we had worked hard to cut back each new incursion, latterly much less effort had been required to keep it in check.

Chambers continued. "Now it's entered into the second phase, combining carbon from the soil with oxygen from the air. I am sure that it cannot have evolved that way, it must have been engineered to suit the purpose so perfectly."

"How long?" I asked.

Chambers shrugged. "Impossible to say. If the same coverage as we see in England and Canada is repeated world wide, we might start seeing global changes within months. Local effects, like in the harbour there, will be apparent much sooner, but even a light breeze would clear out the low-lying pockets."

"Months!"

"The weed might not have taken hold everywhere. The world is covered in deserts, ice-fields, all manner of climates. Who is to say it will be as successful everywhere?"

"If it is engineered, as you suspect, then why would it not be?"

He grimaced. "That's my opinion, as well. Now you understand why our efforts are so urgent."

What, then, would be the point of the weapons we aimed to build? Was the uranium in our hold useless, after all we had endured to retrieve it? At this thought, my confidence in our abilities began to falter. Was producing a bomb going to be enough? Were the Martians even now developing counter-measures to reduce the effectiveness of the blast? Could we refine the mineral sufficiently to produce a weapon at all?

I voiced my concerns to Chambers, hoping for reassurance, but he had none to offer.

"I do not know," he confessed.

"But you pushed for this," I said. "You drove us towards this voyage, this mission, and now you tell me it was all a fool's errand?"

"No!" His eyes flashed angrily. "I believe it is vital, essential, even. We have no other reliable means to bring down a Martian fighting machine, and regardless of the precautions we take, they will eventually discover our Wiltshire base. Just as they found the one in Shropshire, we were so recently forced to leave. If Russell can produce a disease as virulent as the one which saved us the first time, and if he can deploy it past the Martian defences, then we will need to wait for it to spread, and do its work. It will be of no use if they are hammering at the gates and all we can do is hope they succumb before we do."

"So neither method will help us," I said. "We are doomed, after all."

"I can't believe that," Chambers assured me. "We have hope, at least, and that will carry us far. We have scientists, engineers, the very best of us working to develop these weapons, and there is no reason to believe they will fail."

"But you do not believe they will succeed," I pointed out.

He paused before answering. "I cannot know that they will, I admit. But I believe this is not to be the end of mankind. I believe that the Martians underestimate us, view us as little more than their cattle. That is how we will defeat them."

"By being underestimated?" I asked. "They are rounding us up, wiping us out. These are hardly the actions of an enemy who believes us not to be a threat."

"What would you call those labour camps?" Chambers asked. "They put men to work mining something vital to their own operations, something that would be—and will be—an existential danger to them if we stole it. And stole it we did!"

"Armand thought they just didn't want to risk themselves in a dangerous mine," I reminded him.

He waved a hand. "Speculation, nothing more. But even if they were motivated by mere self-preservation, why hand us the means to destroy them, if they believed for a second we had the ability to use it? Because they do not consider us capable."

"Except that we just stole uranium from them. That must alter their opinion of us, surely?"

"Perhaps, or they just think we took it to deprive them of it, with no understanding of its purpose."

"You're placing a lot of stock in this theory," I cautioned him. "What if you are wrong?"

"Then they wipe us out tomorrow," Chambers said flatly. "Humanity's dominion over the Earth comes to an end, and we are the last generation."

"Good God, man! How can you consider such a thing so calmly?"

"Because there is nothing I can do about it. Either we will have a chance to strike back, or we do not. My only option is to be prepared to take the chance if we are afforded it. Everything I have done proceeds from that. If you prefer to believe our continued existence is in God's hands rather than our own, if that gives you comfort, then by all means say a prayer for us. While I continue to draw breath, I shall fight."

"And if, by fighting, you draw their wrath upon us?"

"I am certain we shall. No intelligent being would refuse to fight back when attacked, and so they will retaliate. My goal, one I share with Russell, is to ensure that we injure them so severely that they cannot win. That by the time they realise that we are a formidable adversary after all, it is too late."

I elected not to share the substance of that conversation with Amy. While Chamber's assurances had relieved some of my doubts about our prospects, I was certain that under assault from my wife's formidable mind, my fears would resurface and my confidence would crumble. I decided to take a leaf from Chambers' book, and work towards our goal as if it was the only possible path.

Of course, I underestimated Amy's ability to sense my moods, and within an hour of my discussion with Chambers, she had wheedled every detail from me.

"He's right," she said.

I blinked in surprise. "I assumed you would disagree," I stammered.

"Oh, I think he's too optimistic, to be sure," she said. "But you're too pessimistic. And his analysis makes sense. We can wallow in despair, cry and wail and rend our garments at the death of our species, or we can do something about it. If I am to die at the hands of a Martian, I would have it be while I am fighting back, rather than weeping. And I know the same is true of my husband."

I embraced her tightly. "So much for us not being heroes," I chuckled.

"I meant it as a metaphor, as you well know," she said, pulling free of my arms. "You and I can better serve in other ways than running into battle with firearms and dreams of glory. The cargo we bring, my medical assistance, are both more vital than a man with a gun."

I could not help but wonder what she thought my own contribution would be.

## Chapter Twenty-Six

# Verdict

Searle may not have been permitted to inflame public opinion, but it was clear that the damage had been done already. His suggestion that we had all gained a place of safety by metaphorically clambering over the bodies of those less fortunate had landed on fertile ground. Most people would never accept that they themselves had done anything wrong, of course, but any man who claimed he did not feel guilt at enjoying even the limited comforts of his current situation would be a liar.

Survivors of tragedy, of massive and disastrous events, are often prone to ask, 'why me?' Why did I live when so many did not? Appeals to providence, to God, to some higher purpose are sufficient for some to assuage the guilt, but for others, they never feel worthy enough to have earned survival. Yet others never confront the situation, afraid of peering into the abyss.

When the trial resumed the next morning, the observers filed along corridors with scrawled messages from those who had taken Searle's arguments to heart. One read 'Judge yourself', another, 'Survivors or killers?' One lengthy passageway sported Searle's parting words, ripped from the Bible: 'Let he who is without sin cast the first stone!'

News of the graffiti spread rapidly, and while before long it was removed, the impact was undeniable. There were a number of suicides in the following days, the deceased often leaving behind notes dripping with remorse for their own survival, and committing their souls to God for him to judge.

Some of the bereaved refused to accept the verdict of suicide, believing foul play from one of the 'guilt-mongers' as they became known. From that day forward, men regarded each other with more suspicion. Was my neighbour one of the guilty? Did he think me a killer? Did he think himself one? Would he choose to dispense justice?

———◆○◆———

Against a backdrop of mistrust and fear, the trial continued without further incident. Searle and Wharton were both cautious in their arguments, afraid of causing another uproar. Nevertheless, the arguments were firmly made and deeply debated.

"No matter the situation," Wharton said, "the law is the law. Murder is murder, and handing over men to Martians is the same thing."

"I object!" Searle leaped to his feet. "Exceptions to that law are made regularly. What of self-defence? A man may kill another to save himself."

"Is that your argument now?" Wharton replied. "You believe there was some pact, some agreement between the accused and the Martians, that they were acting out of self-preservation?"

"There is no proof that the prosecution can offer to dispute that!"

Frederick called for silence. "You need to offer the evidence, Mr Searle, not the prosecution. If your defence is one of self-defence, you must convince the jury."

"My clients lost their entire family, your honour." Searle gestured towards the elderly couple, sat mouse-like in the dock. "They only survived themselves because they handed over passing men."

"Mere conjecture!" Wharton exploded. "Not to mention *post hoc, ergo propter hoc*; their survival could have been for any reason, and to assume their actions are the cause is a fallacy. They were elderly, infirm. No Martian would want to make them slaves, or a meal."

"Then why not simply do away with them? Because they proved useful. Their actions kept them alive, thus I claim self-defence."

"Again, Mr Searle, your evidence please?" Frederick asked patiently.

"My client's testimony, your honour. That was their true and honest belief, and the motivation for their actions. They have explained this in their own words, and that was also attested to by the prosecution's own witnesses in their statements."

"A belief that what you do is right is not sufficient to outweigh the offence," Wharton rejoined. "A man who claimed he was drowning a witch would not be acquitted of murder just because he sincerely believed in his own delusion."

"Are you asking the court to rule on the existence or otherwise of witches?" Frederick asked, stifling a smile.

Wharton did not smile. "No, your honour, of course not. But the advocate for the defence is asking it to rule on the motivation of a Martian, something even further beyond our understanding. A belief is not enough, there must be evidence."

Frederick paused for a moment. "I believe, if you will forgive me, that we are arguing in circles at this point. Let us leave this particular issue for the jury. Mr Searle, do you have another argument to make? Do your clients wish to address the court?"

"No, your honour. I would ask the jury to consider the unprecedented times in which we find ourselves as mitigating circumstances, however. They should ask themselves what they would have done in the same situation."

"I say again, the law is the law," Wharton said. "It is not a jury's place to debate what caused someone to murder, but to answer whether a murder was indeed committed. By the testimony of the accused themselves, they sent those men and women to their deaths."

<hr />

Frederick turned to face the dozen men and women at the side of the court. "Members of the jury, you have heard the arguments put forth, and now you must decide the matter. The charge is murder, an unknown number of counts.

"I know that this is an emotional case, but I must ask you to put aside emotion for the time being. The facts, uncontested by either side, are clear: the accused handed over men, women and children to the enemy, knowing full well that this would mean the deaths of every one. What you must decide is simple enough, on the face of it. Does this meet the requirements for murder? If you accept Mr Searle's argument that this was self-defence, that this couple were clinging to their lives in the only way possible, then you must acquit. If, on the other hand, you believe that they were making a choice in their actions, that they were under no imminent fear of death, then you must return a verdict of guilty.

"I ask you now to retire, and consider your verdict. Take all the time you need, debate the matter carefully. You find yourselves at the centre of the first trial of a new age, one which will form an important precedent from this point onwards. Do not take this decision lightly."

The jury filed out, and the court adjourned. The observers, unwilling to risk missing any developments, milled around just outside the chamber, discussing the case among themselves. Everyone who was not required for vital operations drifted as close to the courtroom as they could manage to hear the news at the first opportunity.

Frederick later told me that he did not expect the decision to take long to reach, but he admitted that he was surprised when, only just over an hour later, he received word that the jury's deliberations had concluded.

"We find the defendants guilty on all counts."

Nobody was at all surprised, and a rousing cheer echoed down the halls at the news. A few small pockets of 'guilt-mongers' remained silent, but did not otherwise object. Arthur and Mabel sat mutely, slumped slightly in their seats, but showed no visible reaction.

After order was restored, Frederick spoke with the foreman of the jury. "Was your decision unanimous?"

"It was, your honour."

"Then I thank you for your service, and the jury is dismissed. Gentlemen," he gestured to Searle and Wharton. "As to the matter of sentencing..."

"The prosecution requests the penalty of death, your honour," Wharton interrupted.

"The defence urges clemency, your honour," Searle quickly replied.

"I am curious," Frederick said, "on what grounds should I be generous?"

"The age of the accused, the scale of their losses, the unbalancing of their minds as a result."

Wharton turned to face him in disbelief. "You argued they knew well what they were doing, that they had a pact, now you say they're incapable of understanding their actions?"

Searle stood ram-rod straight, unwilling to meet his eye, fixing his gaze directly on my brother.

Frederick leaned back in his chair and templed his fingers. Silence filled the room as both advocates, the slight figures of the guilty and the massed ranks of observers, waited for his next words.

"Please rise," he said to Arthur and Mabel.

Awkwardly, they rose to their feet, leaning on one another for support.

"Your crimes are heinous," he said. "Though your victims might have gone overlooked in the sheer magnitude of our defeat by the invaders. Every human life is sacred, and these days each one becomes ever more valuable by virtue of its scarcity."

The courtroom seemed to hold its breath.

"I sentence you to spend the rest of your natural lives in confinement."

A chorus of gasps and incredulous cries rang out in the courtroom, and as news spread through the base, distant shouts and groans could be heard.

"The cell you have occupied during this trial will be your home. You will be fed and cared for, but you will never have your freedom. You will also be protected from reprisals by those who do not agree with this court's mercy." He then turned to address the observers and the crowd beyond. "There will be no vigilantes, no self-appointed executioners.

The court has spoken, and the decision is final. Any attempt to subvert justice will be met with the most severe measures."

With those words stunning the crowd into temporary silence, Arthur and Mabel were led away to their cell, and the courtroom slowly emptied.

# Chapter Twenty-Seven

# England

We approached the coast of England with trepidation, under-standable given the circumstances of our departure. The crew of the Minadora were keen to moor even further offshore than before, and neither Chambers nor I were able to convince them otherwise. My protests that the longer their men spent rowing us ashore, the greater the danger fell on deaf ears, and I resigned myself to a slow, nauseating journey back to dry land.

Under cover of darkness once more, we set ashore. Lots had to be drawn to select the oarsmen, so reluctant were the crew to risk their lives. In vain did I attempt to reassure them that any Martians awaiting our return would doubtless have become bored and moved on. In truth, I barely believed it myself, so little could we comprehend the workings of their minds.

In the end, we reached Avonmouth without incident, and the desire of the crew to return to the relative safety of their vessel propelled them to unload the uranium at record speed. I could scarcely bring myself to watch as they manhandled the barrels between teams, fairly pitching them out of the boat onto shore. I was certain one would fall, perhaps crack open, and doom us all. Or perhaps one would slip beneath the waves, robbing us of our best chance to strike back against the Martians.

Before long, the barrels stood arrayed along the waterfront, the Minadora's tender was pitching and rolling its way out to sea, and we found ourselves waiting once more.

"I thought you said our men would be here," I said to Chambers. I shivered and stamped my feet against the cold of the night. Amy was bundled up in my overcoat, and I had pulled on every sweater and jacket I had to keep warm. We all agreed that lighting a fire would be too great a risk, but I was beginning to consider risking it, nonetheless.

Chambers checked his pocket watch for the dozenth time. "I called in by radio, they promised to meet us. I had expected them to assist with the unloading, to be honest. I am just glad the Minadora's crew were as keen to leave as they were and did a quick job."

"We can't carry these things all the way to Wiltshire," I gestured at the barrels. "Some of us could perhaps set off walking, but should we leave our bounty here with a minimal guard?"

"That would be unwise," Chambers said. "If the Martians can indeed detect the radiation, they'd know what we had here. We'd lose it all, not to mention the element of surprise."

Amy's teeth chattered as she spoke. "I imagine that has gone already. Surely the Martians in Canada would have shared the loss with their brothers around the world?"

"Perhaps," I shrugged. "Or they might be embarrassed to have been robbed by such as us. In any case, they can't have known where our plunder might be headed."

"Whatever the situation," Chambers said, "I don't want to lose our prize. Perhaps we can find a hiding place that will delay detection, or even prevent it?"

Searching the dockyard in the dark proved challenging, our small lanterns barely shedding enough light to prevent us stumbling over debris as we explored. Our best option appeared to be a shed or warehouse built from concrete blocks, which Chambers believed might block the radiation from a cursory search. "And the roof is corrugated metal, which might help too," he pointed out, "certainly it would be better than leaving them out in the open. If we run into our colleagues on the way, we can direct them to it."

All hands were set to work transporting the barrels over to their new home. At first we tried carrying them, but we grew quickly tired, and our cold fingers refused to grasp them tightly enough to prevent us from dropping them. Had they been round, we might have simply rolled them about, but our attempts to do so ended almost as soon as they began. The flat sides of the triangular shapes made such a loud clanging sound when they hit the ground that we were sure we'd be discovered. So it was that we were standing around, hands in pockets or tucked under our arms for warmth, staring at a scattered collection of barrels, when the welcome party finally arrived shortly after midnight.

A coded exchange of short and long whistles let us know they were the men we expected, and soon enough, a train of four horse-drawn carts pulled into the docks.

"We were getting worried," Chambers said as the lead man jumped down from the wagon. He introduced himself as Webster and shook my hand limply.

"I know," he replied, "but there was a Martian camped out in a field near our route, and we lost the better part of a day."

"He didn't follow you, I hope?" I asked.

"No fear, we watched him head north and didn't so much as breathe until he was long gone over the horizon. So what are we here to collect? All they'd tell me is that you had something of vital importance, and we had to bring it and you back at all costs."

"It's not for us to say," Chambers said. "But it might well turn the tide." He indicated the barrels, and the new arrivals leapt into action.

"Fine, keep your secrets," Webster said. "But that looks like no metal I've seen before, so I reckon you've robbed a Martian. Any men who can do that are alright in my book."

A cough from Amy alerted him to her presence, and he tipped his hat to her. "Or women," he added sheepishly.

With extra hands, and bolstered by hot tea from an insulated flask, we soon had the barrels loaded. Shortly before dawn, we set off for home.

◄●►

"How have things been since we've been gone?" I asked, as the sun rose slowly above the horizon ahead of us.

"Not great," said Webster. "The trial kicked up all sorts of trouble."

"And the Martians?" Chambers asked.

"They've stepped up patrols, seem to be out at all hours now. There's more of them whenever we transmit, sitting on the high ground."

"Triangulating," Chambers speculated. "Working out where the transmitter is by checking the bearing from a handful of machines. Clever."

"Annoying," Webster grunted. "So far, we've managed to get packed up before they come close, but there's only so many places nearby that we can hide to send messages, so we've had to cut back. And we've pushed out further, widened the distance between the transmitter and the base, but it's only a matter of time before they catch the radio team."

"Or find the base," Chambers said. "I trust you're not operating in a circle around the mine, are you? If they plotted the sites on a map, would it bring them to our doorstep?"

Webster frowned. "We hadn't considered that," he muttered. My heart leapt into my mouth for a moment before he snorted loudly. "Of course we take precautions, we're not morons. We roll dice and toss coins to pick the locations, keep them properly random. Russell has kept us on our toes, don't you worry."

For all Russell's faults, I could rely on him to keep himself safe, and as long as he was billeted with the rest of us, we'd all benefit from his caution.

"But there's no doubt the Martians are looking for us," Webster continued. "Something's changed in the past week or so, and they're not just picking off stragglers any more. If you ask me, it has something to do with your secrets back there." He gestured into the back of the cart. "Midway through your 'mission', everything changes, and we're supposed to think it's a coincidence? No chance."

If true, this would be the first definite evidence that the Martian invasion was being coordinated worldwide. We'd always assumed it had been; that any breakthrough we might make in one territory would impact their behaviour globally. As Webster had said, the timing of this latest change was too close to be a coincidence.

The question was, had they determined that we'd brought the uranium back here?

Evidently, the same thought had occurred to Chambers. "Are they acting differently everywhere?" he asked. "Do you have reports from other nations, for example?"

Webster thought for a moment. "You'd have to check with the higher ups, the rumour mill doesn't cover the contents of the messages."

Could the Martians have recognised us somehow? Or had they worked out that the humans in England were behind the theft? As far as we knew, this was the only place where an atomic blast had happened, so we might be the only ones who had learned of that weakness. The theft of nuclear material might be too great a coincidence for them to overlook.

Then again, if they had pinned the blame on us, why would they not have laid siege to the docks in Bristol? They had seen us leave, after all, and could easily have blockaded the port. They stepped up patrols and attempts at finding our base were worrisome, but they could have snuffed out our resistance before it began, if they had known we were bringing the means of their destruction to England.

So this should be a cause for celebration, surely? While we had brought greater surveillance upon ourselves, the lack of an overt attack must mean that our adversary did not know where the threat resided. The increase in activity must be precautionary, and most likely worldwide, if they didn't know who to blame for their loss.

Unless...

I leaned over to whisper to Chambers. "What if they allowed us to land? Hid themselves, and are watching us even now? We're leading them back to our base, where they can swoop in and reclaim their property, wiping out their biggest threat into the bargain!"

Chambers paled. "Surely not," he gasped. "If they were following us, I'm certain we'd know about it. You can't hide a tripod. If they can see us, we'd see them. Right?"

"What if they can track the radiation somehow? We speculated that might be possible. They blew up that lorry fast enough, after all. They might be able to stay out of sight while we show them to our front door."

There was a long silence as Chambers and I both considered the implications. Eventually, he broke the silence. "We have to know. I'm open to ideas."

I outlined our thoughts to Webster, who sat tight-lipped. I could see the cogs turning in his mind as he considered the situation, before he reined in the horses and drew us to a halt.

"So you think they can track some invisible emanation from these containers of yours?" he said. "And do it while remaining hidden, to boot." He shook his head. "At least you told me about this before we got home, I suppose."

"Do you have a radio?" Chambers asked. "We could call in, find out whether the extra patrols are truly global or just us."

"No," Webster replied. "If using it would just draw them to us, why bother with the extra weight? It probably wouldn't help to ask, anyway. Even if the activity has stepped up worldwide, would you be confident that's not just one of their ploys?" He rummaged under his seat and pulled out a well-worn map. I spotted a rifle barrel poking out from underneath a blanket in the space before he tugged the fabric back over it. "Let me think," he said, and unfolded the map.

Webster's lips moved as he pored over the map, his finger tracing around various landmarks and features. Any attempts to ask what he was looking for were met with silence. The crew in the rear of the cart were growing restless at the delay, and Chambers sent them out to patrol. Without explaining why, he reminded them to look for any evidence of Martian activity.

"And see if you can forage any food," Amy added. "It's late in the season, but fallen apples can still be good if they landed in the leaf litter, and there are always mushrooms. Don't eat any until we've checked for poisonous ones. I used to dry them for use in winter stews."

The men set off, reporting back every few minutes, while Webster continued his scrutiny of the map. Just as my patience was wearing thin, he looked up and fixed me with a stare.

"There's a marble quarry a few miles away as the crow flies," he pronounced. "We might trick the Martians into thinking that's our destination, and draw them out that way." He pointed at the map before sliding his finger over to another point. "We're here right now," he said. "Ideally we'd have turned off back here, but even if they're watching us, they might put our detour down to caution."

"So you intend to drive us into this mine, and then what? Wait and see if they kill us all?" I asked, rather too loudly.

"Not all of us," Webster replied. He kept his voice much more even than I had managed. "Most of us will be hiding nearby, watching to see what happens. I will be expecting someone to volunteer to drive the cart." He looked between Chambers and I in a way that left no uncertainty about who he thought was responsible.

"Hold on," Chambers said. "While I've no doubt that will work, we'd lose the entire supply that way."

"And keep the base," Webster said. "Which is the most important factor, don't you agree?"

"Well, yes, of course," I said. "But there must be a way to test our theory without undoing all that we've fought and sacrificed for, mustn't there?"

"I'm open to ideas," Webster said. "But you'll better have something before we reach the quarry."

Chapter Twenty-Eight

# Quarry

Nothing focuses the mind quite like a deadline. By the time we left the main road, our patrolling soldiers back aboard, Chambers and I had formulated the outline of an alternative plan. All we had to do then was convince Webster that it was better than his own. To my surprise, he embraced it.

Every half-mile or so along the quarry feeder road, we painfully unloaded another one of the triangular barrels, a four-man job without the benefit of a crane. Each was left with a single soldier to guard it, who had strict instructions to hide it as best as he could. Amy dished out the edible mushrooms and berries that had been gathered, having tossed the ones she was uncertain of over the side of the cart.

"Pile earth atop the barrels," Chambers advised. "Even a few inches might mask the radiation sufficiently." Without a ready supply of shovels, this was easier said than done, but to their credit the men set to work scooping the damp earth with their helmets, hands and whatever else they could put to use.

By the time we reached the perimeter fence of the quarry works, we had only two of the containers remaining. The last of the men clambered out and took up hiding places in the area. Now all that remained were Webster, Chambers, Amy, and myself. I had thought of asking for a volunteer among the men, but Chambers had insisted that he be the one to drive the cart inside. "The uranium was my idea," he said, "as was this mission. And so the blame falls on me, if there is any to be doled out."

"Surely you don't wish to be alone," I protested. "I know how solitude and confinement underground can prey on a man's mind."

"Which is precisely why I haven't asked you to join me," he said, placing a hand on my shoulder. "Do you forget I read your memoir? Besides, if we are being followed, I shall know soon enough. And if not, I have nothing to fear. In either case, my 'confinement' will be over shortly."

His voice never wavered. But I knew this man well enough by now to see the fear in his eyes, if only for a fleeting second.

Amy embraced him, which startled him, but he soon recovered and smiled when she told him that she would see him again soon, and called him "a brave soul". Webster shook his hand warmly, giving no more acknowledgement than a tight nod, which Chambers returned solemnly.

"Don't tell Mary", he said, before he cracked the reins, the horse plodded off into the quarry, and the rest of us went in search of a suitable hiding place.

How it rankled to be cowering under a bush while yet another man risked his life for my safety. I suspected I had spent fully a quarter of the time since the Martian return hiding somewhere or other. Given that almost all the first invasion was spent avoiding discovery, I suppose I should have been glad to have enjoyed my liberty as much as I had; but once again I found myself waiting in the wings while other, braver, men took the risks.

The shrubs we burrowed under were all but dead, the coming winter robbing them of any chance to defeat the invasive red weed that had clambered all over them. As I lay there, I was sure that I could sense the toxic effluvia they were pumping into our air, displacing the precious oxygen. My breath grew tight in my chest, and only with an effort of will could I convince myself I was imagining it. We sat atop a small rise, and even if the noxious gas had not been heavier than air, the chilly breeze that tickled my nose and cheeks would have carried it away.

I worked to keep my mind from such thoughts, scanning the horizon around us for the first sight of a fighting machine. Each man guarding a cache of uranium had been issued with a flare, and strict instructions to fire it only if a Martian showed unusual or unexpected interest in the hidden material. At every moment, I expected a flash of red light and a streamer of smoke to pierce the sky, but as time wore on, nothing was reported.

Of course, this might imply that the caches had been overrun, the men taken or killed before they could raise the alarm. Such thoughts did not bear up to scrutiny—the Martians were far from stealthy, and a flare could be sent up in moments—but it says a great deal about my state of mind that day that I was unable to prevent such intrusive ideas from recurring. So it was paradoxically a relief when, after about an hour of hiding, Amy grabbed my arm and pointed off into the distance.

A red flare, dim against the bright sky, hung on its parachute, billowing red smoke.

I struggled to work out which cache it must be, the twists and turns of the road had quite confused me, but it mattered little. Dashing off to intervene would do little good, a handful of men against a fighting machine would barely slow it down.

All eyes were now on the horizon under the flare, straining for the first glimpse of danger. A glint of metal, perhaps, or smoke rising from a fire set by the heat-ray. Maybe we'd see the coils of the black smoke writhing over the ground towards us. With a start I wondered if the Martians might have flanked us—if they could detect the uranium, they would have an idea where we all were—and I scrambled to check all points of the compass. My anxiety did not recede when I saw nothing, but rather intensified. In the same way as a darkened room holds infinitely many more horrors when dimly lit, the lack of any sign of trouble only convinced my fraught mind that danger lurked just out of sight.

At any moment, I was sure, the next flare would go up, then another, and we would have to watch helplessly as all our efforts came to naught. The sea voyages, the loss of half our number before we'd even left Bristol, the sacrifices made by our Canadian allies, all of it would find an end here. Despair filled me, a depth of melancholy I had not experienced since...

Then, a figure appeared. A soldier, waving frantically in the distance. Against my urging, Webster stood and waved back, at which the soldier broke into a frenzied run towards our location.

"He'll lead them right to us," I muttered. "Their orders were to wait for sundown, and we would gather them up on our way back."

"Something has clearly happened," Webster said. "And this man believes it is important enough to break protocol. I wish to hear what he has to report."

"He's scared, is what he will report," I replied. "And he forgot his orders in his panic."

Amy's hand fell upon mine, and she gave it a gentle squeeze. "We are all scared," she whispered, "but he is a professional. Let us hear what he has to say."

The soldier skidded to a halt on the damp earth just in front of our hiding spot. He saluted Webster and stood at attention.

"I'm not a soldier, son," Webster reminded him kindly. "What is it?"

I held my breath. Here it was, the doom we had evaded until now.

"False alarm, sir."

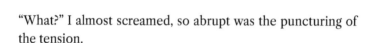

"What?" I almost screamed, so abrupt was the puncturing of the tension.

"Private Simmons, sir," the man gasped between struggling for air. I fought the tightness in my own chest as I thought about the depleting oxygen once more. "He was examining his flare, and it went off unexpectedly, sir. I was near enough I could hear his shouting."

"More likely he fiddled with it," Webster muttered. "Thank you for informing us, Private, but you should not have come. You put us all at risk, sprinting out in the open like that."

His face fell, the thought had clearly not occurred to the man. I had sympathy for him, I knew all too well how it feels to have done something you believe is for the best, only to have the rug pulled from beneath you and realise you have erred.

"Sorry, sir, but the thing is, he's injured, you see?" The man wrung his hands and shifted awkwardly. "The first aid equipment's all still on the cart, and he's burned his hands, and..." he trailed off under our gaze.

For a moment, Webster stood in silence, while the soldier clearly wished for the ground to open up and swallow him. Eventually Webster looked at his watch, squinted into the approaching sunset, and made a decision. "Go and tell

Chambers we believe we're in the clear and he can come back out. Then fetch the first aid kit, and double-time it back to Simmons. We'll make our way back and pick everyone up."

The man snapped off another salute, apologised for it, and darted down the mine entrance as if Webster might pursue him at any moment. We watched him go, and then to my surprise Webster chuckled.

"An injured man is not amusing," I reminded him.

"Of course not," Webster said solemnly. "But a fighting man so terrified of me certainly is. I had no idea I cut such an imposing figure."

I stifled a grin of my own and joined the others in stretching out my limbs. The chill and the enforced stillness had quite caused my joints to seize, and it felt good to exercise them again. Before long, our running man returned from the mine, first aid bag slung over his shoulder, and we all gazed sternly at him as he passed. I swear he accelerated, vanishing into the gathering gloom at a full sprint.

"I should have gone with him," Amy said. "I might have been able to help."

"I doubt you'd have kept up," Webster said. "I'd rather you stick with us than get lost in the dark."

Chambers led the horse and cart out of the mine just as the sun vanished below the horizon. He bore such a look of puzzlement that I almost burst into laughter, but managed to control myself.

"Who was that?" he asked. "Fellow came charging in as if pursued by the hounds of hell, gabbled something about burned hands, snatched my bandages and bolted. He barely had time to bellow 'you can come out now' before he was gone, but still managed to call me 'sir' three times. I imagine he's in the next county by now."

Amy, Webster and I could hold in the laughter no longer. Chambers' perplexed look only intensified as we doubled over, wheezing and crying. Once we caught our breath once more, we clambered aboard, Webster took the reins and I explained the situation to Chambers.

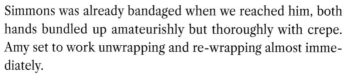

Simmons was already bandaged when we reached him, both hands bundled up amateurishly but thoroughly with crepe. Amy set to work unwrapping and re-wrapping almost immediately.

Loading the barrels back into the cart was a lot harder in the dark, and with one fewer pair of hands to assist, it was heavy work. Tired arms and weary minds are a recipe for injury, and I consider us fortunate that, the unfortunate Simmons aside, we all came away with nothing more than a few aching muscles and one twisted ankle.

Even without the strenuous activity, the excitement of the day and the length of the journey would have rendered me exhausted. The combination of all these factors conspired to have me unconscious within minutes of loading the last barrel. Amy later told me I snored like a cart-horse.

I awoke some time later, but the near pitch blackness around me threw me into utter confusion. For a moment, I thought

I was already back in the Wiltshire mine, in the windowless bed-space carved from the rock. Then the rocking of the cart convinced me I was at sea, before my barely conscious mind decided I was buried alive, back beneath the earth thrown over me by the crashing cylinder of the first invasion. That last thought caused such a panic that I almost jumped from the cart before Amy could restrain me.

"Hush, darling," she whispered, "we're almost home. You're safe."

Her calming words did the trick, and I glanced about to see the watery light of the lantern hanging on the traces of the cart, barely illuminating the way ahead. Memory rushed back, and I knew where I was.

I took solace in knowing that the other men around me could not have seen my panicked reaction in the darkness, that Amy alone was aware due to her proximity to me. I idly wondered whether they were also troubled by nightmares or terrors such as I had been before the cart drew to a halt. Webster's voice sounded from the driver's seat.

"Hallo!" he cried, and I shrank back against the sound. Such a loud noise, after so long sneaking about, seemed dangerous. I realised he was hailing the guard of the base, who responded in a similar fashion.

"Who goes there?" came the shout. Then, curiously, a single word. "Shirt."

"Collar." Webster answered without hesitation.

"Proceed," said the guard. That had been some sort of password, I assumed. The cart lurched back into motion, and we continued on our way. Around me came the sounds of men waking, stretching and grumbling about their discomfort, and I looked forward to a decent meal and perhaps a hot drink.

# Chapter Twenty-Nine

# Changes

I was able to enjoy the hot drink, at least. The meal, a bath and a decent night's sleep would all have to wait until Russell was satisfied with our debriefing. Had I been in his shoes, I might have only been concerned about the uranium, but he barely gave the barrels a second glance before he had shuttled us off to the cavern that passed as a meeting room.

Chambers rushed off to reunite with his family, and so I was forced to recount every incident of our travels at least once, and often twice or more, so that Russell could form a clear image of events in his own mind.

"The sick Martian," he pressed, long after the teapot was drained dry. "What were the symptoms?" He levelled a finger at me. "You saw them the first time around, close up, did it look to be the same disease? Something new?"

"I am no doctor, or veterinarian, or whatever manner of physician would deal with their anatomy. And the only ones I saw last time were already dead and decaying. This one looked... miserable."

Russell laughed. "I doubt it was dying of malaise, dear boy. I need specifics. Did it sneeze or cough? Was it hot or cold, shivering, febrile?"

"I didn't notice any signs like that, and I don't know whether the one I touched was hotter or colder than normal. It might have been dying of old age for all I could tell, or internal injuries. We only assumed that it was disease because they succumbed to it the last time they came. I haven't contracted anything, and I was doused in the creature's foul blood."

"I suspect there is also more than a little wishful thinking," Amy added. "We want to consider them as sick, vulnerable, fragile."

Russell ignored her. "Perhaps the blood sample will tell us more," he huffed. "I ought to get to work."

I rose from my chair to seek out dinner, but he waved me back.

"Before I do," he continued, "there is another question."

"I believe we have told you everything we know," Amy said pointedly. "Twice."

"It will only take a moment," Russell protested. "You mentioned you did not become sick after exposure to the Martian. Were there any illnesses among the men, even before you ran into that beast? Anything untoward, unexpected, unusual?"

"More unusual than your concern for a fellow man's well-being?" I spoke before thinking and swiftly apologised.

Russell shook off the insult. "You've had a long day, and a trying time," he said. "Do not take my prioritisation of my work over the concerns of other people as heartlessness. But did you notice anything strange?"

"Other than my husband becoming sea sick almost immediately, and headaches due to poor air at the docks, we were blessed with good health for the entire journey," Amy said. "So I believe we are done here." She stood, grasped my arm, and almost hauled me out of my chair.

I stammered some sort of farewell to Russell, while Amy led me at speed towards the canteen.

I ate mechanically, barely tasting the food. I could not have told you what it was, so exhausted had the day left me even before Russell's interrogation. More than once I found my eyes closing of their own accord, my fork half way to my mouth. After my knife clattered to the floor, Amy suggested it might be time for bed, and I shuffled along behind her towards our sleeping quarters.

Even though I knew full well that my lethargy was due to my tiredness, and no other cause, Russell's concerns about sickness had wormed its way into my mind. Memories of the splashing Martian blood covering my hands and face caused bile to rise in my throat, and only the greatest effort of will could drive panic from my heart.

Whether our beds had been used while we were away, or kept empty against our return, they had fresh, crisp sheets upon them, and blankets that were less musty than the ones we had tucked ourselves under while aboard ship. In truth, they could have been threadbare, filthy and damp, and I would probably still have clambered in and slept as deeply as I did that night.

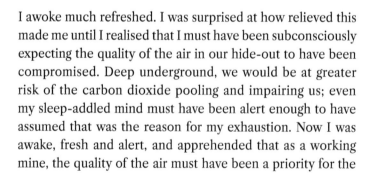

I awoke much refreshed. I was surprised at how relieved this made me until I realised that I must have been subconsciously expecting the quality of the air in our hide-out to have been compromised. Deep underground, we would be at greater risk of the carbon dioxide pooling and impairing us; even my sleep-addled mind must have been alert enough to have assumed that was the reason for my exhaustion. Now I was awake, fresh and alert, and apprehended that as a working mine, the quality of the air must have been a priority for the miners. No doubt they knew more about keeping a supply of oxygen flowing than I did.

After a hearty breakfast, I joined Chambers on his way to supervising the unpacking of the first uranium barrel. The area designated for the work was in the deepest part of the mine, furthest from the entrance, and would take us a while to reach.

"Would you not want to be nearer fresh air?" I asked him. "Or outside, perhaps?"

He shook his head. "If the Martians can detect this material, the deeper the better. Besides, the ventilation for the entire mine runs through here."

"Won't that spread it?" I asked in alarm.

"The air flows from the rest of the place into this room, and out through a natural chimney and fissures in the rock. Anything that gets out of our control poses no risk to the facility."

The chamber where the barrels were stashed was at the far end of a short tunnel. The entrance was well-marked with warning signs and posters, and secured with a steel gate. Two armed guards flanked the opening, and one nodded curtly at Chambers as the other opened the gate.

Once we had squat-walked our way along the low corridor, we arrived at what Chambers called the supervision area. This contained a few folding chairs and desks, each of which had seen the lowest few inches of their legs removed, to better fit in the confined space. Chambers greeted a couple of men who were sitting in front of a chalkboard covered in formulae and symbols I did not recognise, before leading me down yet another low tunnel. This twisted back and forth before opening up into a vast, echoing cavern.

At the very centre, dwarfed by the surrounding space, stood the small collection of the triangular barrels we had risked and lost so much to obtain. One was separated from the others, and had two men working gingerly at it with pry-bars and hammers.

Both wore an over-suit crudely stitched out of white cotton, along with a pair of stout boots and a white cotton balaclava, which formed both a face mask and head cover. As they looked up to see who we were, light glinted from goggles that covered their eyes. All told, they looked unearthly.

"We do not believe there is any real hazard," Chambers explained, waving them back to work. "The miners had been exposed for hours at a time with no short-term effects, after all. However, the barrel contains a concentration of ore greater than would be found in the earth, so it doesn't make sense to take risks. My primary concern is dust, hence the protective clothing. We can prevent its inhalation, and the suits can be removed and cleaned here, so nothing is brought into the other caverns."

A metallic sound indicated that the lid of the barrel was now loose, and the men removed it, placing it carefully on the ground beside them. One now brandished an instrument above the opening, from which a rapid clicking sound emerged. As he drew the instrument down the side of the barrel, away from the opening, the clicking slowed, and then accelerated again as he aimed it inside.

"Three hundred", the man called, and set the device aside. With a pair of fire-tongs, he reached inside, pulled out a greyish lump of nondescript rock, and placed it carefully into a metal bucket. He worked quickly, placing a lid on top, before he and his colleague replaced the lid of the barrel as well. One more pass with the clicking device, and they appeared satisfied. One man brought the bucket over to an array of impressive-looking machinery along one wall, while the other delicately placed the tools into a wooden box alongside a variety of other implements.

Their work evidently completed, the two men then walked over to a large hanging sheet between the entrance area and the machinery. One stood about a foot in front of it, raised his arms out to his sides, and slowly turned upon the spot, while the other aimed a set of bellows at him, blowing at his thin cotton suit. Once the first man had completed a full rotation, they traded places, repeated the curious motions and then stripped off their outer garments, placing them into a large metal bucket. They then passed the clicking device over one another, apparently to their satisfaction, before wishing us farewell and leaving the room.

"The sheet is treated with glue to capture any dust," Chambers explained.

"And that device?" I asked. "It measures the activity of the uranium somehow?"

"Yes, someone in Manchester before the invasion figured it out. The particles ionise the air, and that allows an electric charge to pass through. We render that as a click, and the more clicks, the more radiation."

"How many clicks are too many?" I wondered aloud. "And it's still doing it, have we had a spill?" The device was ticking away merrily to itself, once or twice a second.

"No, nothing to worry about," Chambers assured me. "There's always a little activity in the background, especially underground. We're still working with animal studies to establish a safe level, but for now we're just cataloguing what each man is exposed to, and keeping it as low as possible."

"These men are still taking a risk," I said. "I trust they are fully aware of the dangers, and are volunteers?"

"Of course," Chambers confirmed. "But they have balanced the certainty of our destruction by the Martians if we do nothing, against an unknown peril."

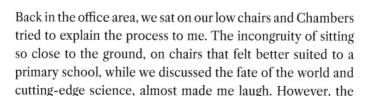

Back in the office area, we sat on our low chairs and Chambers tried to explain the process to me. The incongruity of sitting so close to the ground, on chairs that felt better suited to a primary school, while we discussed the fate of the world and cutting-edge science, almost made me laugh. However, the topic was deadly serious.

"The scientists who studied this stuff previously made a few key findings," Chambers said. "Purifying the uranium is only the first part of the challenge. Once we've removed it from the other minerals in the ore, we're still left with a blend of isotopes."

"Equal... place?" I translated.

He nodded. "You know about the periodic table?"

I did not.

"It's how we classify the elements, each one in its place. There are some elements that have two different masses, but are chemically identical. We call them isotopes, since they occupy the same place on the table."

"Different masses?" I queried. "By what measure? Surely a pound of one is a pound of another?"

"Each atom," he replied. "A single atom of uranium can weigh either 235 units, or 238. A unit, in this case, being an atom of hydrogen."

This was all passing well above my head, and I told Chambers as much.

He chuckled. "It doesn't matter, apart from to say that we need one and not the other for our purposes."

"And so the difficulty becomes separation," I said.

"Exactly, like someone mixed sand in with sugar, but at the level of individual atoms. In that case, we could add water, dissolving the sugar, filter out the sand and then dry the sugar out to separate them. But in this case, the two act the same chemically, so there's no suitable equivalent. The only difference is the mass."

"So, how will you tell them apart?"

"We have a couple of options. Heavier atoms will diffuse through a membrane more slowly, for example. Or a centrifuge can spin the heavier ones to the bottom of a vessel, leaving the lighter ones above. And we're exploring a new method, using magnets to nudge them around, so the heavier ones go one way and the lighter ones another."

"It sounds like you have it well in hand," I said, my head still spinning.

Chambers looked sheepish. "We've got a lot to do," he admitted. "The part we need is under one per cent of the total, and for our purposes, we believe it must be nearer twenty per cent."

"That's a lot of sand in your tea," I mused.

# Chapter Thirty

# Cattle

While Chambers and his team continued with their labours, I was glad of the chance to get away from the ever-present clicking of their radiation meters. No manner of assurance was sufficient to allay the fears that every tick of the speaker was another second, minute, or hour stripped from my life. While the much more familiar dangers of disease were no easier to push from the forefront of my mind, I resolved to visit Russell for an update on his progress.

His own facilities were also burrowed deep into the cave system, no doubt for similar reasons of safety. Everyone knew where they were, and I was given directions whenever I needed them. Often the instructions were accompanied by a smirk, and I could only assume that it was rare for someone to seek out Russell's company.

As I rounded one corner, I discovered that I was mistaken in the source of their amusement. In a side-cavern, behind a thick rolled fence of barbed wire, stood a truly bizarre sight. The floor of the space was lined with red weed, freshly cut by the looks of it, and emitting that disquieting metallic scent. Munching on the waxy leaves and stems was... some kind of animal.

My first impression was of a malformed cow, perhaps some birth defect having vastly increased its girth and reduced its legs to mere stumps. The leathery skin in a rust-red hue told me, however, that this was no earthly creature, but another invader from Mars. It had a vast, near-cylindrical body about three yards long and maybe one across, with stubby limbs along the sides. Three were visible on the side nearest to me, and I assume they were paired opposite. While thick, they must have been insufficient to bear its weight on this planet, since they splayed out across the top of the weed in an almost comical manner. As I watched, it wriggled them obscenely to draw its mass forward a few inches in order to reach fresh leaves. I suppressed a shudder at this apparent blend of insect and mammal, though whether such distinctions existed on Mars, I had no idea.

The rear bore no tail, and the front end terminated in what I suppose I must refer to as its head and neck. Protruding from the cylinder of the body was a mass of muscle around a foot across, with no discernible shoulders. It was not possible to draw a line between the neck and the head, either — at one point the face appeared, with no visible distinction. I could see no ears, and the mouth was surrounded by tentacles. These were much shorter than the similar ones I had seen on Martians, presumably being perfectly well suited to drawing sustenance towards the bare hole with a triangular lower lip that served as mouth. Atop all of this were three eyes, large and spaced around the head so the creature could presumably see in almost every direction at once. Much in the manner that prey animals on Earth evolve eyes on either side of their head, this one had taken the idea to extremes. The concept that there might be something that preyed on this creature that had forced it to evolve as such distracted me enough that I did not hear Russell stepping up beside me.

"Magnificent, isn't she?" he said, and I fairly jumped, to his amusement.

"What is it?" I breathed, unable to take my eyes off the creature.

"We're calling it a cow, for want of a better name. 'Mars-cow' might be more accurate, but it does sound rather foolish, don't you think?"

I nodded dumbly. "Where did you get it?"

"Captured on one of the supply runs," he said. "The Martians have been turning them loose all over lately. I'm surprised you didn't see any on your trip."

Could I have I overlooked them in fields as we went past? Had my mind simply filtered them out, assuming they were stray cattle escaped from a farm? No, it was hardly the sort of thing I'd miss, I had to admit. Then again, we'd been so focused on other matters, and so exhausted, I had to concede I might not have been looking so closely.

"Come on, we can talk in my office," Russell said, leading me away from the curious beast, and before long, I found myself staring at another frightening selection of warning signs.

"Pay them no heed," Russell waved as he welcomed me into his empire. "They serve to keep the riff-raff at bay, but there is no real danger."

"Should I take that to mean that you have made no progress during our absence?" I asked, taking a seat in his erstwhile office. A cane, no longer needed now his leg had healed, leant up against the thin plywood partition that separated him from the rest of his team.

An expression of hurt flashed across his face before he caught himself. "We have made great progress, I assure you. But science is not done by flashy breakthroughs or miracle discoveries. It's a slow, steady process, one of eliminating false ideas and dead ends."

"I hope that the samples we brought will help," I said. "I'd hate to think we risked ourselves in vain."

"Oh, I'm sure they will be invaluable," he agreed. "I have men growing cultures from them as we speak; if there is some malady that we can use, I assure you we will find it."

"And you have one of their cattle now," I pointed out. "Something you can test it on."

He looked shifty. "Indeed," he said. "Although it's already dying."

"Surely that's good news!" I exclaimed. "That's the goal, after all."

Russell shook his head. "It's not ill, or at least, not infected. If I didn't know better, I'd say it was pining away."

Were the Martians' cattle social animals? Perhaps they roamed the landscape in packs for protection from that predator I had imagined, and had evolved a collaborative nature as a result. Unlikely, I reasoned. That curiously shaped head left little enough space for a complex brain, and while ants and bees might be social here on Earth, they lacked any understanding of community, working purely on instinct. No bee has ever lapsed into depression upon being separated from the hive; no ant has wasted away from loneliness.

"We've given it food, the same leaves as it was eating in the wild. And we offered it water, although it seems to gather everything it needs from the red weed."

"Perhaps some trace element," I mused. "Some additive to the soil that the weeds gather and transfer into it."

"Not one we can discover," Russell said. "Whatever it lacks, we're at a loss to detect it in the soil or in its food. No, it's malaise stems from another cause. "

*Malaise*, I thought. From the French... and harkening back to a time when illness was thought to be caused by bad smells. Now, of course, we knew that diseases were transferred by bacteria or viruses, and not polluted air. Hence Russell's work, of course.

"The air!" I shouted. My outburst must have startled someone beyond the thin partition, as the sharp smash of a glass vessel echoed through the cavern. "Tell me, is there fresh air in the creature's habitat?"

"Of course there is," Russell barked. "The entire complex is ventilated thoroughly. I supervised the selection of these chambers to ensure the air came to us as cleanly as possible."

"Therein lies your problem," I said triumphantly. As best I could, I reminded him of Chambers' theory about the conversion of our planet's atmosphere to better match that of the Martian home world."

I could see the battle behind Russell's eyes. The scientist within him clearly appreciated the theory and could see how it explained his observations. The other part of his nature sought to reject any idea that he himself had not originated. For a moment I wondered which might win out, before he sprang to his feet and barked orders at his underlings.

They brought heavy cloth sheets, soaked them in pitch to make them as air-tight as possible and then hung them across the entrance to the cow's prison. With the light breeze that passed through the corridor thereby blocked, ventilation would no longer reach the creature. Russell sketched some equations on a clipboard, estimating respiration rates and the effect of the red weed before pronouncing that the animal would be on the mend within a couple of days.

"It makes sense," he proclaimed, once all his orders had been attended to. "We captured this one in a valley. Most of their grazing grounds are low-lying — we just assumed they were ill-equipped to climb the hills in our gravity. It must have been since the carbonic gases settle there."

"They'd certainly struggle to climb," I said, "but it sounds as if they were deployed where they'd have the easiest time of breathing as well as foraging."

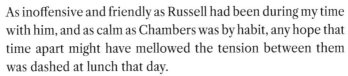

As inoffensive and friendly as Russell had been during my time with him, and as calm as Chambers was by habit, any hope that time apart might have mellowed the tension between them was dashed at lunch that day.

"You're wasting your time, and what is worse, the time of good scientists," Russell barked, spitting mashed potato across the table. "Purifying, enriching, concentrating, whatever you call your process, it's doomed to failure."

"Nonsense," Chambers retorted, at a more reasonable volume. "We've had some success already. According to our readings, we've more than doubled the concentration."

"Which you need to repeat, what, tenfold? It's a fool's errand. Those men should be working for me, refining our virus. Blowing up the odd fighting machine isn't going to win this war, we need to strike at the base of their food chain."

I waded in before I could stop myself. "Are those men's skills suitable for such a task?" I asked. "Surely there is no overlap between the study of the atom and of diseases?"

Chambers sat back, his arms crossed, and grinned at Russell, who glowered at his plate for a moment.

"Science is science," he eventually muttered. "Any *decent* scientist can turn his hand to anything."

"It strikes me that your own team are seeing little success," Chambers said. "I've not heard of any breakthroughs, or seen piles of dead weed for all your trouble."

Russell turned as red as the tomatoes on his plate. "We have only just received your samples of Martian biology, as well you know, and it takes time to culture."

"And we have only just received the samples of uranium," Chambers rejoined. "You have had weed a-plenty since the first weeks of the invasion, and that strange beast almost as long as we were gone."

I interjected before they came to blows. "So perhaps we should reserve our judgement until both teams have had a chance to work, gentlemen?"

Chambers refused to let the matter lie. "He's had the red weed for months, and talks of attacking the bottom of the food chain. Kill the weed, starve the cattle, kill the Martians; a laudable goal, but one he is no nearer to achieving than he was before they arrived."

"We've tested innumerable strains," Russell said, "and some showed remarkable promise. One was extremely virulent, in fact, but did not distinguish between Martian and Terran biology as well as we had hoped. Fortunately, the mice we used let us know before we moved on to human trials."

"Human trials?" I queried. "You intend to test this disease on us?" Russell looked much more sheepish than my request warranted. His eyes darted from me to Chambers and back again, never quite meeting our own. "Or have you already?"

Chambers gasped, and Russell blanched. "It was necessary," he stammered. "If we are to release a pathogen, we have to know it is safe to use and won't wipe us out along with *them*."

"Which poor souls did you convince to risk themselves? I hope to God you rewarded them for their bravery."

"He probably just volunteered some poor chap from his science team," Chambers said bitterly. "One of the ones he didn't feel *decent* enough."

Again, Russell refused to meet our eyes.

"Who was it?" I asked, quietly. "Oh God, did they die?"

"I just pray you didn't let it spread to the whole base," Chambers said. "Kept them confined while you studied them."

EARTH UNDER THE MARTIANS

"No, they didn't even get a sniffle," Russell snapped. "And they were isolated, of course. They'd either have died of it or recovered before they reached another human being."

*Before they reached... No, he wouldn't have.*

"The ship," I whispered.

"I could hardly do it here," Russell protested, "if it had swept through the base we might have lost everything."

"I don't understand," Chambers said. "What did he do?"

"He gave it to us," I snapped. "How did you do it, lace our food?"

He shook his head. "I inoculated your clothing, placed it deep into your luggage so you wouldn't be exposed until you changed. That way I could be sure it wouldn't escape until you were safely aboard the ship. If anything had happened..."

"We'd have vanished without a trace," Chambers said through gritted teeth. "You'd have chalked it up to the ship sinking, or a Martian attack, or who knows what, and carried on as if we'd never existed."

"It would have been perfect," I said. "He'd get rid of the chief proponent of the atomic weapon and allow all resources to be directed at his own pet project."

"You should be court-martialled," Chambers growled. "Then taken out and shot. I volunteer for the firing squad." He was shaking, his knife and fork clattering on the plate until he threw them down in disgust and stood up. "You're finished, Russell." He spun around and strode from the room.

Chapter Thirty-One

# Ultimatum

Chambers had not banked on the changes of opinion which
the trial had caused in the shelter. I had only just learned of
the divisions the proceedings had caused, and even I assumed
that a new trial for Russell would be immediately ordered.

Frederick, however, was reluctant.

"You were not here," he admonished me. "You didn't see
men turning on each other, see the partisan battle lines that
were drawn up. And that was merely over whether the death
sentence was permissible or not. Their guilt was never in
doubt by either side, and still they divided us."

"Then take capital punishment off the table," I urged. "Even
as one of his possible victims, as one of those so nearly affected by the traitors, I do not believe it is justified. Without
that..."

Frederick shook his head. "There are those that will still
call for it. Merely ruling it out would provoke them to who
knows what end. And you assume that Russell's guilt is as
clear-cut and obvious to all."

"He admitted it!" I cried. "And what's more, he's unrepen-
tant. Put him on the stand and he'll boast of his crimes!"

"He has been busy while you were away, gathering supporters. Everyone is painfully aware that humanity is on the
ropes now, and his idea that 'any means necessary' should be
employed fell upon fertile ground."

"Within reason, I would agree too," I said. "Risking the lives of the few of us who remain does not seem 'necessary' nor justifiable."

"Do you believe you could convince him of that? Some of his followers are as fanatical as him about his research, if not more. I have had delegations visiting me regularly, asking for the prisoners to be turned over for research purposes."

"Russell is asking for them as test subjects?" I gasped.

"The delegations say they're acting independently, but I suspect he's pulling strings. In any case, these are the kinds of people from which I will have to draw a jury."

"They'd be clearly prejudiced and rejected by the prosecution. Or manipulate the draw," I urged. "Eliminate his followers from consideration."

"He'll have planned for that," Frederick said. "There'll be supporters who play it safe, don't express opinions, against just this eventuality. We pass them for the jury, then they manipulate the decision behind the scenes."

"So he gets away with it?" I asked. "Just carry on as if he never attempted murder?"

"Murder is a little harsh. He was testing a variant of influenza, as I understand it."

"Which kills people every winter," I shouted. "Not to mention that his 'variations' are designed to kill Martians and his test wanted to ensure it wasn't going to wipe us out alongside. He knew it was a possibility! Why else did he arrange matters so we were aboard ship?"

"Which is where we can agree. His experiments are dangerous. That's how I intend to handle this."

"Exile?" Russell bellowed. "You would send us out there to fend for ourselves?"

We had met him in his research offices, judging them distant enough from the main body of the caverns to offer us the necessary privacy. I was wondering now whether we could ever be far enough from the rest of the survivors for his voice not to carry.

"Relocation," Frederick corrected him calmly. "In light of the dangerous nature of your research, not to mention the recent... safety concerns, we are no longer comfortable housing your experiments in the same location as the remainder of humanity."

"One more slip, accidental or otherwise," I added, "and the Martians will no longer have to trouble with us."

"If you think I can do my work in a tent somewhere, or some farmyard barn, you're mistaken!" Russell said. His eyes swivelled madly, lighting on each of our contingent in turn. Frederick had brought a handful of burly men in case of trouble, though at my request they were unarmed. "That's even assuming the Martians don't spot us immediately and wipe us out!"

His research team had given up all pretence of not eavesdropping by this point and had gathered around us rather too closely for my comfort. Their utter silence was unnerving, and I just hoped that they had faith in their leader's ability to argue their position. If they resorted to violence, we were vastly outnumbered.

"We can do better than that," Frederick assured him. "I know of a place where work was proceeding before the Martians' arrival. It's safe, secret, and well-appointed."

"Why was it abandoned, then?" Russell asked. "And if it's so ideal, why am I just hearing about it now?"

"Who said it was abandoned?" Frederick said.

For once, Russell was silent.

"I have never been a fan of putting all of my eggs in one basket," my brother continued. "You were working in Shropshire, Chambers in London, and there were other teams scattered around."

"I had no idea," Russell stuttered.

"By design."

"But now you want to gather all your eggs in one place?" Russell asked.

"When you had your own location, far from the rest of us, secrecy and dispersal made a lot more sense. Now you're a danger to our survival, it's time to get a bigger basket."

"I'm the means of your survival," he protested.

"You were not the only gentleman working on the spoils of the first invasion, no matter how much you like to believe you might be."

"I don't see anyone else making progress," Russell retorted. "Least of all, Chambers, with his futile attempts at a weapon. Why isn't he being cast adrift also?"

Frederick and I exchanged a glance. "He's our next stop," I confirmed.

Chambers took it better than Russell. He even admitted that he had been surprised at how readily his work had been accepted into the caverns.

"I was expecting this, sooner or later," he said. "Once people got wind of our work, and the dangers involved..." He shook his head. "Of course, we wouldn't do anything we weren't confident was safe, and would never risk anyone without their knowledge." His voice had an edge to it that left me in no doubt to whom he was referring.

"Naturally," Frederick said. "Nevertheless, if I am to relocate Russell for safety reasons, I cannot ask people to tolerate another, potentially greater, risk."

"Where are we to go? And for that matter, where is Russell headed? Somewhere I can't hear him bellowing from, I hope."

Neither Frederick nor I spoke for a moment, and Chambers instantly realised why.

"We're going to the same place, aren't we?" he sighed.

"We lost contact with the other research stations," Frederick explained. "Probably just radio interference, but they're too distant to send you and all your equipment. Porton is the only one within decent travel distance. Besides, it's the best equipped, even if their focus is not on the atomic."

"Porton Down?" Chambers asked. "Wasn't that a chemical research station, if I remember correctly, before the war?"

"They were studying the black smoke," Frederick confirmed. "Still are, although I can't say they've made a lot of progress. Samples were hard to come by, and the chemistry involved is as far beyond us as ever, I fear."

"How have they survived so far?"

I couldn't fault Chambers for asking.

"Some portion of luck," Frederick admitted. "And careful precautions against being discovered. They also make use of caverns for housing now, and they tell me they've disguised their laboratories to avoid drawing attention."

"And the arrival of two additional teams of scientists, plus their families, won't draw attention? Or prove impossible to house?"

"I'm afraid that families might need to remain here," I said.

Chambers' face fell. So recently reunited with his wife and children, and now we were asking him to abandon them once again.

"How far is it?" he asked quietly.

"About forty miles," Frederick said, and Chambers brightened considerably.

"So visits are still possible!" he said.

"Absolutely, although precautions must be taken to avoid revealing either location," I agreed.

I could only wonder whether the latest change in location would be the last. Amy and I had come a long way from our comfortable life in Woking, now so distant a memory as to belong to another lifetime. Firstly to Shropshire, then under fire we had made it here to Wiltshire. Here we had hoped to remain, albeit with a detour to Canada. Now another part of the county beckoned.

"Why would you not remain here?" Chambers asked us when we told him of our plan to accompany them. "Your brother could use your help, I am certain, and I know only too well the pull a distant family can evoke."

"My concern for my brother is assuaged, seeing him so well and so entirely in his element," I explained. "And if you have learned anything of my talents, you know where they can best be applied."

"The fact that Russell and I have ever been able to occupy the same room proves that," he chuckled.

I smiled. "So I should accompany you, to ensure that the situation might continue. In light of Russell's recent activities, I can only hope to keep him in check."

"I had hoped you might keep my wife company," Chambers said to Amy. "Although she assures me that she has made some friends among the few young mothers here."

"She has more in common with them than with me," Amy agreed. "Although listening to her plans for schooling gives me hope for the future, my own talents can be better used in Porton."

Indeed, the only reason Amy would be allowed to live there was that the site had need of nursing staff. While every precaution was being taken in the handling of our putative weapons, the possibility of an accident was ever-present. Should the worst occur, a medical staff on site would be invaluable. There were also animal experiments being carried out, and while veterinary and medical science were formerly distinct disciplines, the reduced number of both meant that an 'all hands on deck' approach was required.

I myself was only permitted to go by virtue of my brother's orders. Frederick had appointed me his deputy to oversee Porton, a role I could not claim any expertise in. I had demurred at first, unwilling to accept a role by nepotism, until he had convinced me otherwise.

"I trust you," he had said. "And more to the point, so do Russell and Chambers. If, God forbid, they come to blows again, then they will respect your decisions. There's no other man here I could send who could make that claim."

"But I know nothing of the details of their work, not the science behind it!" I had protested.

"So they will explain it to you in simple terms, and you will explain it to me more simply still. Anyone capable of understanding it should be working on it and not overseeing. We have not the luxury of appointing experts as middle-men, or promoting a scientist until he does no more science but writes reports all day and night."

So it had been decided, Amy and I had value in Porton Down, and would accompany the exodus of scientists and engineers just as soon as it was arranged.

Each evening, shortly after dusk, a small convoy of horse-drawn wagons set off carrying a handful of men and a selection of equipment. They rode through the night to Porton, unloaded their precious cargo there, and returned just before dawn.

Russell, naturally, had insisted that his own team be the first to transfer. No-one had any objections. The prospect of his noisy protests being relocated sooner rather than later appealed to all, and Chambers gracefully conceded that his own work could be shuttled over afterwards.

By the end of a week, enough of Russell's team had been transferred that no more useful work could be done in the existing labs, and he rode at the head of the convoy that night to take up his new offices.

A tangible calm fell over the bunkers with the removal of the last of his samples, something Frederick and I discussed over dinner that night.

"It might be our best hope for victory," he said, "but I, for one, won't miss having it on our doorstep. I do not envy you needing to keep him in check."

"I make no apologies for what he did," I replied, "but I think he saw a chance to test in what he believed was a safe manner, and let his enthusiasm take charge. Such an opportunity will not arise again, and he knows he will be monitored more closely as a result."

"You are more forgiving than I would be under those circumstances. Learning that he had put you and Amy into danger, no matter how slight he believed it, had me seriously considering the ultimate punishment."

"You would have had him executed?" I gasped.

"I thought about it," he admitted. "But just as with those two old fools, to make an example of him would serve no purpose. And don't forget that we do have need of him and his expertise. But believe me when I say my blood was boiling. If you had pressed for it, I might have agreed."

My head spun. If I had wanted Russell to pay for his crimes, Frederick would have arranged it for me. I thought back over my words, my complaints since learning of his betrayal. Had I given some sign, made some hint, however innocuous, that might have led my brother to take action?

Frederick regarded me with amusement. "Relax," he said, "I have done nothing. You proved yourself able to forgive, and since you will be the one living alongside him, I chose to follow your example."

"I had worried you'd arranged for his cart to meet with an accident," I confessed. "Something deniable yet decisive."

"It would have been simple enough," he admitted, "but that is not how I would want to handle matters. I cannot preach democracy and the rule of law, and then 'disappear' people in the night."

I was surprised to feel relief at his words.

Chambers' labs took longer to transport. We wished to take no chances of discovery and still feared that the Martians might be able to track the uranium. As such, small amounts were shuttled over each night, along with the necessary shielding to keep the caravan drivers and workers safe.

By the time the last of the equipment was loaded aboard the final convoy, it was almost Christmas. Plans were afoot for a festive celebration; 'a vital effort for morale', as Frederick put it. With the resources available to us, however, the preparations were necessarily muted. Paper chains festooned every room and corridor, formed from cut-up pieces of old reports and documents. Some bore smudges of black ink that had been used to redact sensitive information once they had been deemed no longer vital and donated to the festivities.

A stockpile of candles had been produced; while they were not needed for day-to-day illumination, their warm flickering glow did lend a cosier aspect to the bunker that I for one quite enjoyed. The constant temperature underground rendered an open fire unnecessary, although I had always enjoyed the ritual of making the first one of the winter. Having the chimney swept, laying in a supply of wood or coal, and watching the first tendrils of smoke climbing upwards. I hoped that our new accommodation might feature a fireplace, even as I knew that using it would run the risk of discovery.

"Are you sure you won't stay for the party?" Frederick asked, as I clambered aboard the final wagon.

"We shall have our own," Amy assured him, "with our new colleagues."

"What better way for them to come to accept their new supervisor," I joked. The two bottles of brandy that Frederick had slipped me, now tucked safely into my luggage, would do an even better job of that.

"Stay in touch," Frederick urged us. "And take care."

As we pulled out of the quarry, the first flakes of snow began to fall.

# Acknowledgments

First of all, those beta readers who took the rough draft and told me what was right and wrong: Kay, Denise, Nicole, thank you. Thanks also to Maureen for the name suggestions, and Sam for constant cheerleading and support.

My awesome critique group, author circle, whatever we call ourselves – your support and encouragement was vital to the completion of this story, as was your criticism and butt-kicking. It literally couldn't have existed without you. Adam, Darren, Jan, Lynne, Tara: thank you.

The Bestseller Experiment Academy and Facebook Group, a source of wonder, challenge and support like nothing else I've found online.

Martyne, for being a rock and a sounding board – this is for you.

Anyone I've inevitably forgotten, or whose tiny interactions kept me motivated. Thank you.

And thanks to you too, reader, for taking a chance on this book.

# Can you help me out?

Thank you so much for reading this book, and I'd love to know what you thought of it.

Reviews are vital for an author, not just so we can find out what people think, but because it also helps more readers like you find the books they're going to love. So please do consider leaving a review on Amazon or GoodReads.

# Also By Mark Hood

**War of the Worlds Sequels**

Amy's Journal (website exclusive)

The Return of the Martians

Earth Under the Martians

Final part coming soon.

**Fae Defence Society Series**

Jacob's War

The Fairies Want Me Dead

Book 2 coming soon.

**Tales from the Treehouse Anthologies**

A is for Apple - contains my short story Skin Deep

B is for Beauty - contains my short story West of the Moon

# Get your free book!

# About the Author

Mark Hood is an author living and working in the English county of Shropshire which allows him plenty of opportunities to stare out of the window at gorgeous scenery when he ought to be writing.

A life-long fan of science-fiction, classic and modern, he has long been an admirer of H. G. Wells' writing. This series of unofficial sequels were sparked by wondering what we might learn from the Martian technology, and how that might allow us to prepare for the invader's return.

He also brings a life-long fascination with mythical creatures and ancient legends to his fantasy writing, which merges folklore and myth with the real world.

Find out more at https://markhoodauthor.com/ or reach out on Twitter @markhood

Milton Keynes UK
Ingram Content Group UK Ltd.
UKHW021526270824
1399UKWH00081B/2253

9 781913 442231